The Delicate

MATTHEW SANDERS

D1738585

Bloomington, IN Milton Keynes, UK

authorHOUSE

AuthorHouse™
1663 Liberty Drive, Suite 200
Bloomington, IN 47403
www.authorhouse.com
Phone: 1-800-839-8640

AuthorHouse™ UK Ltd.
500 Avebury Boulevard
Central Milton Keynes, MK9 2BE
www.authorhouse.co.uk
Phone: 08001974150

First published by AuthorHouse 6/15/2006

ISBN: 1-4259-3643-1 (sc)
ISBN: 1-4259-3644-X (dj)

Printed in the United States of America
Bloomington, Indiana

This book is printed on acid-free paper.

"'I'll be judge, I'll be jury,' said the cunning old Fury:
'I'll try the whole cause and condemn you to death.'"
- Lewis Carroll, *Alice's Adventures in Wonderland*

About the Cover Artist

The cover images are by Lynn Turner, whose work primarily stresses personal, spiritual, and cultural desires and memories. The artist currently lives and works in Seattle, Washington and can be reached at lynnieat@yahoo.com

Acknowledgments

It's always hard to begin thanking people for any form of work because you don't want to forget anyone in the process. Here's my best attempt. First, I have to thank my boys, Jeremiah and Adam; they are constant reminders that dads need something their children can remember them by.

Thanks to my parents for constant moral support throughout my life.

A great thanks to fellow writer, Christopher Szatkowski, for the endless, invaluable, mind-bending hours of editing and to Lynn Turner for graciously making the cover to this book. A special thanks to anyone who has taken an interest in my writings over the years; just to name a few: Charles McCormick and Mary McCormick (my grandparents), Jason Young, and my Aunt Becky.

Ten years ago, during my junior year in high school, I gave a few poems to my friend to accompany a picture of Kurt Cobain (I'll openly admit I was a Nirvana fanatic) she drew for the school's literary magazine. Only expecting one to be chosen, I was pleasantly surprised to see almost all of them in the publication. The following year I submitted a few poems and a short story on my own accord. When I purchased a handful of copies for family members, the woman selling them asked my name. When I told her, she became excited, saying she read and enjoyed my poems from the previous year's publication and specifically looked for my writings in the second. I would like to thank this woman, although I don't know her name and probably never will, because she was the final persuader for me to continue writing. It made me realize writings can be timeless, something people young and old can associate with; I figure I'll continue this stint as long as people are excited or moved by things I write.

For Jeremiah and Adam

The brown, steel-toed boot caused Truman to fall.

The second blow broke his nose.

His body struck the ground limp. A marionette whose master severed the strings. He was a pile of discarded bones laced with bloody linens. The alley was wet from rain, and clouds built over the city, thunder shouting threats across the sky.

Scattered trash cans and scurrying rats watched Truman's fall as neglectful transients left the dank alley seeking shelter from the oncoming storm. Auburn-drenched moonlight and sky-soaked haze caused the shadows to come alive.

He lay alone, vulnerable, and unconscious.

The cartilage in his nose caved, popping sharp and abrupt, echoing into his childhood, sending him back to his parents and memories he thought he lost. He did not return to birthdays or stories told to him as he lay snuggled beneath the covers. He returned to a cherished moment of his parents giving him sheets of bubble wrap. When they received packages in the mail he would stand near, hands held tightly together in anticipation, silent and wide-eyed, trying to guess if the air pockets on the wrapping were large or small. His parents opened the boxes in his direction giving a forced frown. Styrofoam. His sturdy shoulders slumped as he walked away. When there *was* wrapping, he snatched it from his mother or father's hand and headed out the door, not returning until nightfall.

No older than seven, he ran about the streets with his friends, popping the wrapping, pulling the trigger of a gun. All of the kids met under the second streetlight north of his house, each bringing their own treasure for battle. Snap-Caps received the greatest awe, their realistic gunshot sounds coveted by everyone in the group. These were scarce. Most mothers frowned upon things promoting violence.

Truman and his friends battled anyway, their violence unleashed at an early age. They took turns playing hunter and hunted, the designation usually determined by a quick, mindless game of "rock, paper, scissors".

Truman always chose rock.

The rules of the game often changed. The only requirement was the hunted to give a dramatic death. The difficulty of the game was finding hiding spots not previously used. Living in a small town, this was an arduous task.

The hunter snuck up, weapon of choice in hand, and, when close enough, let loose. The hunted self-administered seizure movements with each pop, finally falling with the dispersion of ammunition.

An act of delicate grace.

Bodies fell to the ground, war-torn soldiers, as the hunter stood over, admiring their kills. Sometimes, a person added a few twitches after he lay still.

Truman was not as graceful during real attacks.

Unlike childhood games, his body did not twitch. His friends would have been immensely displeased with his performance. The blood flowed freely from his nose. With the blood so went the memories. Some entered his mouth, flowing into the street, making a path down his face like a river cutting through stone. The faded brown boots quickly moved back as the blood flowed toward them. It had already turned into a large puddle, covering the alley.

It's hard to decipher blood from rain puddles in the dark.

A second set of boots, slick black, stepped through the blood.

Truman's jaw shattered.

The feet stood still, waiting for movement, bloody tips only inches from his face. The assailant reached down and wiped his boots with gloved fingers. The alley was quiet. With each blood drop, the puddle spawning from the face increased in size, spreading toward the hiding shadows.

After a few moments of stillness, the first set of boots made a nervous motion to leave but halted when the second set began kicking Truman. The methodical, pendulum movements violently connected with different parts of his body.

The hesitant assailant approached but did not strike.

The black boots were too involved to hear sirens bouncing off the walls. The kicking ceased with the tugging at his arm. The assailant stood still; once the siren registered, the boots ran.

Truman lay unconscious, blood bubbles escaping from his mouth.

Dr. Moore

Edward and Christopher lifted the stretcher into the ambulance with ease. As the night progresses there will be grunts from each man, their muscles strained and tired.

Edward disliked Christopher's trivial outlook on life. He usually chose to look out the window, watching the passing street lamps, deferring any possible conversation. He tried to keep his eyes on the outside world, ignoring Christopher, but they drew back, tongue to canker sore, at the mangled body on the stretcher.

"Poor guy," he blurted.

Edward ran his hand over his rock-marred face, following the curvatures of bone.

He imagined himself lying on the stretcher.

Christopher responded, "No shit. Someone worked him over pretty good."

"I've never seen a person who's taken such a beating still be able to breathe. . . " Edward trailed. "If I took a beating like that I don't think I'd want to survive. His brain is probably mush."

"Molmy."

The word resonated above the traffic.

Edward looked around then down to Truman.

"Did you hear that," he asked, leaning into Truman.

"Molmy."

Christopher, unimpressed by the action, sat against the vehicle wall. In mid-yawn, he asked, "What did he say?"

"It sounds like Mommy."

"Mommy?" Christopher was silent for a moment. "Well, I don't blame him. If I got an ass kicking like he did, I'd be asking for my Mommy too."

Edward looked up, giving an unconvincing smile. Christopher looked down to Truman, "Don't worry friend," he looked at Edward, "we'll get you to your Mommy as soon as possible."

"What's his name?" asked Christopher.

Edward grabbed a wallet from the tray and pulled out a driver's license. "Truman Cooper."

Christopher tore it from Edward's fingers, "He sort of looks like that one actor, the one who played the assassin. Shit. What's the name of that movie?" He looked at Truman's pulverized face and smirked. "The picture doesn't look anything like him."

Edward did not give Christopher the satisfaction of a response. He rummaged through the wallet but found nothing.

"They took everything but his license," said Edward.

"Really?"

Edward saw the wheels churning in Christopher's mind, trying to form a witty, or even semi-intelligent response. "It's like they wanted us to know who he was."

Christopher grabbed the wallet from Edward's hands and filtered through it. After finding nothing, he sighed with disappointment then threw it at Truman, "Here you go, bud. Don't spend it all in one place."

It took Edward over five years to numb the feelings violence bestowed. He no longer had the empathy he felt he should, only thinking of the people as another part of his work. An endless routine. As they wheeled Truman to the operating room, both gave pleasant nods to doctors and nurses. When he first started the job, he was in tears after a night's work, seeing the constant disregard for life: children beaten by parents, homicides, suicides, guttings, castrations, the list was never-ending. No matter the circumstances, the outcomes were simple: life or death.

The arrangement presented an ongoing paradox, which ultimately made him void of emotion. Pushing Truman down the linoleum hallway, Edward droned out noises, concentrating on the squeaking wheel of the stretcher and the hum of the lights above. He wondered if the sounds were constant or only heard if people listened for them. Unfortunately, the question was an unanswerable, hypothetical mess.

Gliding aimlessly, Edward relied upon Christopher to steer them in the proper direction; he did not notice as Dr. Stuart walked beside them, spitting questions.

Edward heard Dr. Stuart say, "Thanks guys, we'll take it from here."

A changing of the guard.

From some hidden corner, two young men came and took their places. Edward stood motionless in the middle of the hall. He probably would have stayed there all night had Christopher not nudged him in the ribs.

"You all right?"

"What?" Edward shook his head, "Yeah."

"Let's get out of here."

"Sounds good."

Exit to face further tragedies.

Edward gazed over his shoulder to the empty green hallway. This occurred every time he left a hospital, the necessity birthing from his childhood, from spending ample time in hospital waiting rooms. The length of his stay depended on the beating his mother received from her boyfriend. Bruises mended with peroxide and bandages. But, in more severe and unfortunately all too common situations, she stayed overnight. The threat of internal bleeding quietly passed the lips of doctors, all thinking Edward was too young to understand, instead wanting him to immerse into the cartoons in the waiting room. He watched them for the opposite reason. He knew the severity of the situation and tried to find an outlet of humor.

At twelve, Edward was led out of the hospital for the final time. He knew his mother would not return. It was then he first looked over his shoulder. The doors opened in front of him; darkness pierced his eyes. A dutiful relative (was it his uncle, or was it a cousin?) held his hand. Edward hoped to see his mother turn the corner, arms open wide, running toward him to grab and never let go.

The hallway was quiet and motionless.

When Edward dropped off patients he gave one last look behind to see if he dropped off life or death. He knew the person would not turn the corner but was in the profession long enough to know how each story ended. Destitute or hope was at the end of the hall. It was his last shred of humanity.

Edward knew Truman would live.

He also knew something in Truman disappeared.

What is it, Edward wondered.

Years of life?

Satisfaction?

Redemption?

Edward looked over his shoulder for the last time, afraid of what might be following him.

It was years before Dr. Daphne Moore and Dr. David Stuart began their late night meetings at cheap motels. Thirty-nine, ninety-nine for an entire night. They dared not ask the cost per an hour.

With thoughts of his wife and children behind, David fell to the daunting of a younger female.

Daphne.

Her shapely body.

Mascara-suffocated eyelashes.

Desires are a ticking bomb.

Truman Cooper was Daphne's first official patient. Looking him over, she thought of her previous purpose: to learn. Many times the learning involved hands-on care, but more importantly, she was taught how to handle patients under the different circumstances presented. When she started working at the hospital, her head was full of ideals and compassion, like all new doctors, and likewise, she had an undying desire to save lives.

David watched Daphne intently, knowing it would only be a short amount of time before everything would become too much for her to bear. Too many promising doctors left the profession, tails dragging on the floor behind.

David studied the x-ray of Truman's jaw.

He gracefully ran his capped red pen over the film, his mouth making small, indiscernible words.

Daphne watched his lips and cheekbones, biting the corners of her mouth with each word he spoke, suffocating short, audible, orgasmic gasps.

David turned to her for some sign of understanding.

His forearm contracted.

He had asked her a question.

She dumbly shook her head.

David turned back and studied. Mouth movements. Daphne incessantly nodded her head in agreement, unknowing that he had not asked a question.

He pulled the x-ray off the board.

Flap.

Echo.

He grabbed another film and placed it over the light. He drew an imaginary circle in the approximation of the patient's nose then switched it to one of Truman's hips.

His brow furled. "If he lives . . . endless rehabilitation."

Intermittent phrases sunk into her mind.

He took the x-ray off the board and placed it in the envelope, *Truman Cooper*. The label was an hour old, curling at the edges.

His words began to register, "Get him cleaned up. Suture his jaw. I'll have Dr. Storm assist. Since he lost so much blood, start a transfusion. Check his chart, I think he's type O positive. We'll need to put him on a ventilator in case..."

Daphne anxiously shook her head.

He looked at the envelope in his hands. "I hope you're prepared to deal with things like this."

She did not know how to respond. Through all the hard work of medical school and internships, she always displaced the moral aspect of what she saw with each patient. Not only was this implied in college classes, it was also voiced by numerous doctors and nurses. Everyone she had spoken with said to keep an outside view of the patients because there would be times of lacking right or just answers for what happens. The consensus: too much vested sympathy equaled a doctor who would not survive. She was told not to search for the answer to the question: "Why?"

Daphne stood dumbfounded.

Noticing her awkward pose, David said, "I'll check up on the situation in a couple of hours."

Pondering.

Daphne walked toward Truman's room, thinking of David.

Evolution from lust?

Something new.

A reminder. Father patting her head, as he always did when arriving home. He hunches over and picks her up, carrying her to the dining room where Mother has dinner served. She holds onto her doll's arm with dear life, watching the limp body sway with each step. In a few years he will be too weak to carry her, only minimal strength to lift his arm. He tried, usually resulting in an ill-attempted flopping of his hand on her head.

Post relationship's dissolution.

Melanie had not heard from Daphne for days and after incessantly knocking on the front door, she climbed through a window.

She knocked lightly on the bathroom door.

No answer.

The door was ajar. Slight luminance.

Melanie pushed the door open.

"Daphne?"

The shower curtain was drawn. Melanie reached out with a trembling hand, pulling it aside.

Daphne lay in the bathtub, her body motionless. The slits in her wrist were diagonal, scorned lovers lying in bed, occupying the same space but distance enough to embody the area with solitude. Her blood saturated the water, creating a pink tint, a child's water colorings...

Sloppily drawn apples...

Roses.

Strawberries.

A red-drenched sunset.

Melanie screamed.

Bodies in black surrounded the hole in the ground. The coffin rested above. Melanie did not want to watch it lower; she would never be able to ride an elevator again. She looked away. A mysterious woman lingered in the trees in the distance, pulling dead branches aside to catch a view.

Melanie looked at the surrounding human handkerchiefs and easily slipped away.

She crept up. The woman's body jerked from the tap on her shoulder.

"Why don't you join the rest of us?"

The woman turned, "I wouldn't be welcome."

"Did you know her?"

"Not personally."

"Through a friend?"

"An acquaintance."

"I knew Daphne her entire life. Acquaintances usually involved handsome men molding her into naked, unfathomable positions."

The woman turned away, "I know her through an acquaintance."

"...and may God not punish her for this unforgivable act. This sin." The priest's words drifted to them.

"Nice and uplifting," spat Melanie.

She turned to the woman, "You're her, uh," said paused, "the doctor's wife."

"Yes."

"Why would you want to come to this? I can only imagine..."

"I don't hate her."

"Give it time. Wounds fester and ooze without proper bandaging."

"What's that supposed to mean?"

"With Daphne dead you will only have an apparition for your hate. It will build up, making you want to despise. Not your husband, who'll you'll probably stay with for the sake of the children. You'll have to tolerate him. She will be the logical one to detest... but then you'll feel guilt because she's dead, wondering how you could feel such contempt for someone who you can't even confront."

"You seem to have it all worked out."

Melanie lit a cigarette, "I've been there before. I told Daphne to keep her pants on. Married guys aren't something she should be getting mixed up with. Sexual encounters were play dates to her, nothing more."

"Actions of a whore."

"Maybe. What would that make your husband, then?"

The woman fell silent.

"See. Hate's already surfacing. And then there's the bullshit you're probably dealing with from your husband. Pleading. Begging. 'It was not until I was with her that I realized what was wrong with my life,' that's what one of my boyfriends told me. Cheating sack of shit."

"If you're such a good friend of Daphne's, why are you over here, hiding in the bushes with her lover's wife?"

"Things are more interesting over here," Melanie replied, " Daphne wouldn't want it any different. She was always a glutton for drama."

The crowds began to disperse. The coffin magically disappeared. Melanie flicked her cigarette, "I should probably get back. Good luck to you, I definitely wouldn't want to be in your shoes. Sometimes death unleashes demons that otherwise would have stayed hidden."

Melanie winked as she left, leaving the woman helpless behind the foliage.

Daphne made a dutiful attempt to do what David would have wanted. When a patient had multiple injuries as Truman did, it was a very timely effort, and her goal was to have David commend her. He will walk into the room, see the sewn shattered jaw, and in his modest tone, say, 'Masterful'.

Of course, she had to settle with, 'Good job'. Even with the slight and impersonal comment, she blushed as she walked away.

Daphne walked to the attending nurse, "Did you have someone call the police?"

Julia sighed, "Never matters in these situations. As long as I've been here, I don't think there's been a successful attempt at finding the person."

"Maybe we can find out who he is."

Julia grabbed a wallet sitting on the table and handed it to Daphne. "That's about all we know."

Julia applied the cast to Truman's leg.

Daphne opened the wallet.

"Only a driver's license?"

"Yeah, he lives in town."

Daphne looked at the picture of Truman then at the body lying in the hospital bed. He was handsome in the picture, vibrant green eyes, a small nose with slits for nostrils and soft skin. He had a well-trimmed goatee and slightly sunken cheeks below prominent facial bones. She studied each detail, in turn studying the converse of his present self. In mere minutes, Truman Cooper transformed to something unsettling. She casually tapped the license, "Truman Cooper."

"Your Truman Cooper appears to have had a rough night."

Daphne did not appreciate the humor.

"Please make sure the officer gets this," she said, placing the wallet on the table.

When Officer Lancaster arrived at the hospital, he sponged all of the dictated information into his child's-sized notebook. He tried to hide the Pooh Bear and Piglet cover from Julia. The characters were in a questionable hug. He always felt Piglet had ulterior motives with Pooh Bear but Pooh was too simple to catch on. He scrawled Julia's words with sick indifference. After each sentence he proceeded with a complacent "Okay," or a long sigh. After Julia gave all the information, Lancaster snapped his wrist, closing the notebook. He put it in his front shirt pocket. Julia knew his candor came with hours of practice, envisioning him standing in front of a mirror at home, shirt off, tofu-colored gut curling over his Dukes of Hazard belt buckle.

She grinned.

"Oh," said Julia, "I almost forgot. He's been mumbling 'Mommy' since the medics picked him up."

"Mommy?"

"That's what it sounds like. It's barely audible. Pretty difficult to understand a person with a broken jaw, wouldn't you agree?"

Lancaster made motion to his pocket but quickly pulled his hand back, "That's some pretty crucial information, don't you think?"

"I suppose, if his mother's name is Mommy Cooper."

His face turned beet as he headed for the exit. Just before walking through the automatic doors, Julia saw him pull the notebook from his pocket. It did not take much effort for her to guess the five letters written, most likely all capitalized: MOMMY.

Smoky - undoubtedly named for the stench rising from his clothes-scratched the unshaven mess on his chin, "Cooper? I know him. Pretty quiet. Goes to work and comes home, sometimes with a woman on his arm . . . on good nights. Yeah, never had any problems with him."

Officer Lancaster wrote everything, giving Smoky a slice of importance on his toothless face.

"Did something happen to the guy?" said Smoky.

"You could say that."

"The only reason I ask...I have a list of people waiting for a open apartment. Good, solid money. Now, don't get me wrong, I'm not heartless," Smoky stopped abruptly. "Did he die?"

"Not yet."

"Car accident?"

"Assault."

"No shit. Did they find the son of a bitch that did it?"

"The perps haven't been found," Lancaster looked at the notebook, "How long has he been living here?"

"I'd say about two years."

"Do you know where he came from? Names of relatives?"

Smoky thought for a moment.

"Nah, nothing like that. Let me pull his application. There's always some references on that."

Smoky headed to the back office.

Lancaster was reluctant to follow but found comfort in the firearm strapped to his waist.

A sheet of smoke filled the room. On the desk were two ashtrays full of cigarette butts, tightly compressed, distinguished with fury. Smoky sorted through papers.

He grumbled and slammed drawers.

"Here we go."

He placed the application on the desk. "No luck. He left the area blank."

Lancaster stretched his neck, trying to grab a glance of the document. Smoky saw the attempt. He lifted the paper with a smug look on his face, 'I wasn't lying, cocksucker'. Lancaster gave a nod of approval; Smoky let the paper fall. He pushed his chair back from the desk, defeated.

"He put a sizable deposit down," said Smoky. "That's the only way I overlook references. Money speaks for itself."

"So you've insinuated."

Lancaster applied the period to his final sentence with a swift movement of his wrist then closed the notebook. "Thank you very much for your time. Please give me a call if you hear anything."

"You know, his rent's due next week and if he's not..." Smoky trailed. "I'll put his stuff in bags, in case he doesn't make it."

Daphne stood over Truman's unconscious body. The ventilator and rhythmic vital signs echoed in the empty room. The noises had a serenity to them. Daphne toyed with notions of sleep. She had visions of the same room a few days before, full of passing nurses and doctors, each with a certain job to perform, each accomplishing their job: keeping Truman Cooper alive. She opened her eyes to the empty room and looked at him. Her lids twitched and body weakened at the knees. She braced herself with the bed. Her hands wrapped around the support, nails digging into her palms, knuckles becoming the metal bars encasing Truman's motionless body.

What's the purpose, she wondered.

Would Truman have been better off dead in the dark alley?

David quietly walked into the room as Daphne pondered the never-ending questions.

He spoke like a parent talking to his child, "It'll get easier."

She wiped a tear.

"I don't know if I want it to."

He put his hand on her shoulder, the first physical contact between them. "Well, then you'll be better at this than I thought. I take it no information was found on him?"

"They went to his apartment and spoke with the owner, but there was nothing about relatives or friends." She sighed. "They couldn't even figure out where the guy works."

"I see."

She looked at Truman, then to David, "So what do we do now?"

"If he stays like this, we'll have to transfer him with the other comatose patients. They're in Glacier Falls. It's a medical center about ten miles from here."

"Will he come back?"

"There's always a possibility."

"Can you give me a straight answer?"

David studied her face, finding the inability to read her expression intriguing.

She asked again, "Do you think he'll wake up?"

"No," he responded mildly.

"That's all I needed."

She walked to Truman, leaned over, and gently kissed him upon the head, her lips touching an endless line of stitches.

Angela

Alexander shook the raindrops from his jacket. The drizzling turned into an onslaught, drenching him as he walked to work. He dried his feet to the best of his ability on the tattered mat at the entryway. The squeaking of his shoes echoed off the beige walls until he stopped at the front desk.

Kristin briefly looked up from her fashion magazine.

"Good morning," said Alexander.

"Mmmhhh."

"Anything exciting happening?"

She rolled her eyes.

"I'll take that as a no?"

Knowing Kristin was through conversing, Alexander walked the hall. Kristin assuredly said, "Angela was looking for you," as he rounded the corner.

He did not give her the satisfaction of turning around.

"Thank you Kristin," he stated.

He felt her eyes upon him, her mouth devious. He held his path, not to see her again until the end of his shift.

Alexander entered the room whistling.

He made his way to the window, "How are you doing this monotonous morning?"

He opened the blinds and the glass, which clanged against a metal pole. Hospital regulations. He stuck his nose in the six-inch opening and took a whiff of the wet air.

"There. That should get rid of the stuffiness." Alexander said slyly, "and maybe the hospital smell. Not going to say hello? Maybe tomorrow."

No longer in casts or bandages or with stitches covering his face, Truman lay still like a sleeping newborn. Alexander pulled down the sheet.

"It's been raining all night and this morning. I slept with the window open," he paused, "Never turn away the smell of fresh rain . Words to live by. I'm still waiting for snow but I'm not going to hold my breath."

He massaged Truman's left foot, "It's funny, you drive an hour in any direction and there's snow, but we never get any ourselves."

He concentrated on his massaging, switching to the right foot. "Guess I can't complain though. I grew up in Phoenix."

He walked to the window and watched the rain. "It's nothing like this place. Not much green there. We had to add colors to life on our own." He mused, "I do remember this one time it snowed. I was about eight, and it was freezing. One misconception people have is that it never gets cold in Phoenix. During the winter, it was cold enough to put frost on our car windshields. Hell, we always used our fireplace around Christmas. But we paid for pleasant weather with the summer months. Anyway, this snow came down; it wasn't much, mind you, but it was enough to remember.

"I would say it had been about three months since my father left. I was a walking zombie. I didn't know which way was up and which was down. It's strange, when a person doesn't have much color around them, it makes things harder to understand. It wasn't until the snow that I put things into perspective. I allowed the flakes to fall on my head. Cold shots of reality. I remember Mom yelling at me from the doorway to come inside but there was something more important going on. I must have been standing there for close to an hour, until the snow turned to drizzle. It was only nature and I. When I finally was able to move, I no longer felt what I had been for the past three months. No blank, contemptuous thoughts.

"Actually, the uneasy feelings invaded my life much earlier. Living with my parents allowed me to feel the tension they did. Children always know more than their parents think they do. I was cleansed from that moment on, at least until…"

He heard someone enter the room.

"Alexander, do you really think the cold air is good for the patients?"

"It can't be worse than the stuffiness." Alexander shrugged, "At least we don't have to deal with the smell of death."

Dr. Jeffery Fine pulled a clipboard from his side, a gunfighter in a shootout, his clipboard his weapon. "So, has there been any progress with Mr…."

Jeffery trailed off and flipped through the pages. It always bothered Alexander when doctors had not learned the names of patients, especially patients who had been in their facility for close to a year. Although Jeffery wanted Alexander to save him from the embarrassment of himself, Alexander said nothing, letting the doctor struggle.

There was a sigh of relief, ". . . Cooper."

Alexander rolled his eyes, "Nothing worth noting. Only unsuccessful attempts at preventing bedsores."

Jeffery frowned and cleared his throat, "Yes, well, has he said anything? Any noises? Any movements? Wiggling of fingers or toes?"

Alexander did not answer.

Jeffrey blew air heavily through his nose, "Alexander?"

"What's that?"

"Mr. Cooper. Is there anything new with him?"

"No."

He made a few marks, letting the papers flop. *Slap.* Jeffery pulled the clipboard to his side, tapping it against his hip, standing with a nervous tick in his right leg, a helpless child waiting for his parent to take him to the restroom.

His eyes fell on a small Christmas tree in the corner.

"Do you bring those in for all the patients?"

The tree had no presents underneath and only a short strand of black and orange lights loosely strewn around it.

He shrugged. "Only those without families."

"Nice gesture."

"I figured everyone should have some sort of decorations. There's a person locked inside. A prisoner unable to free himself. Trapped. Probably hearing voices in a small amalgamated room," Alexander leaned into Truman and whispered, "I think they're hearing everything we say, absorbing it. That way, when they wake up, they'll know. Would you be comfortable if they remembered everything you said?"

Jeffery cleared his throat and walked over to the tree, lifting up the strand with his middle finger. The lights fell, slightly shaking the branches.

"Halloween lights," said Alexander. "Clearance. Ninety-nine cents."

"I think you're giving them too much credit. Don't get your hopes up. In many cases like Mr. Cooper here, the question is whether the mind is still working. He took a severe beating. In working with comatose patients, I've never seen someone wake up from something like that."

"If I was to take that outlook, I don't think I could come to work each day, knowing I've helped them stay alive for what appears as no purpose."

"And what if these people's existence is to make others realize that nothing should be taken for granted? What then?"

"It's still a purpose. However, if one of these patients were to wake up after all these years, for no other reason than to make *them* realize *their* life was being taken for granted," Alexander paused. "I want to be there when it happens. More can be learned from that than the usual trivialities of life."

Jeffery did not argue. He quietly walked over to the bed and looked down at Truman. "Did they ever find his family?"

"No. He appears to have been a loner."

"A shame. In seclusion and no one comes to visit."

He shook his head and exited the room.

Alexander returned to the window.

"You had your monthly visit from the doctor."

Musty air breezed through the small opening.

"The trees are so green. A color that could never be fully captured on canvas," he paused. "At least, not with justice. It's too pure to be confined. Clean. Natural.

"One day, when you wake, I'll take you on a walk, so you can feel openness . . . something different from your current concrete prison. I wonder if you've ever done something like that? Enjoyed nature?"

He walked back to the bed and fidgeted with the pillows under Truman's head, "Kristin said Angela was looking for me. She's the one I have a date with this weekend. I think I talked about her before; actually, she's tended to you a couple of times when I was sick. I follow her sometimes, when she leaves work. I am a voyeur but it's nothing deceitful. I can't help but appreciate the slighted glances she gives Kristin every evening, and how she eats alone every night at a coffee shop down the street, reading Dostoyevsky or Pasternak. But not Doctor Zhivago. Spectorsky. An apropos, inviting choice, at least for me. Her face . . . I've always believed a woman's face is their most important physical attribute, seeing it's something you'll have to look at the rest of your life. Everything else changes. Boobs sag, asses drop and get bigger, but a person's face usually stays the same, aside from wrinkles for posterity to look upon as wise.

"It's crazy, we haven't been on a date and I'm already putting a lot on her shoulders, like we're going to spend our lives together. Here's to hoping, I guess. I'll tell you how it goes."

Uncomfortable situations.

Alexander's guarded portrayal, though not well-received by membranes of the opposite sex, was a regular act. Chiseled, sporty features and sensitive lines were his best attributes. Aside from patients, he did not speak to many people at his work; he believed it was his quiet approach which sprung interest in Angela. Women thought his quietness equaled homosexuality, which Alexander found most intriguing, especially with each of them pursuing dates on the notion. A conquest, he assumed.

It was rare for Alexander to go on a date, and usually unheard of for him to consider someone he worked with. He made an exception for Angela. She appeared sincere, which was an attribute he thought only existed in the quiet individuals he cared for.

Thinking of sincerity's link with silence put a smile across his lips. He wished more people abided to such a standard.

"What's so funny?" said Angela.

"Huh? Oh, nothing."

Angela did not pursue the matter. She quickly learned earlier in the evening that any conversation with Alexander would be an arduous task, and she wanted to save the deeper questions for subjects she controlled. She picked up her fork and took a small bite of the steak, chewing it close to twenty times, only stopping because there was nothing left to chew. She repeated. Alexander watched as she performed the ritual. Up. Down. Up. Down. Her jaw made quick movements. After three pieces of steak, sixty chews, he leaned across the table and quietly said, "It's really not necessary to do that."

Unaware he had been watching her, Angela deeply swallowed a fictitious piece of meat, wiped her mouth, and said, "What?"

"The proper etiquette. It's not necessary around me. I don't believe that you chew your food to nothing when you eat alone."

She blushed.

"And I've seen you reluctantly eye the basket of bread on numerous occasions, but you've yet to take a piece."

He picked up the basket, "Don't be shy."

She hesitated then tore the bread with her teeth. She rubbed her hands together, discarding the crumbs from her fingertips.

"Do you mind intrusive questions?" she asked.

"As long as you can handle shocking or upsetting answers."

"What could be so upsetting?"

"Depends. What are you asking?"

She straightened. "Okay. I really want to know why you chose the line of work you have. You're good with the patients. You have a very soothing, gentle way about you. It's as if you're supposed to care for people."

"This wasn't always my profession of choice. I had a different aspiration for life . . . it didn't pan out. Sometimes it's not what we want, but what is preordained."

"That's caustic. Why? What did you want to be?"

"Nothing important."

"If it wasn't important, I don't think you would have wanted it to be your career. So what is it? What did you want to be?"

"An artist. Paintings. Stuff like that."

"An artist? I could see you being an artist. You have that look."

"What look?"

Alexander fidgeted in his seat.

"I don't know," she responded. "That arty look. You know what I mean."

He wiped sweat from his brow, "I'm sure I don't."

"So what made you stop?"

He did not want to answer but the words swelled in his stomach, ran up his throat, and passed across his lips, "My mother..."

"What's that? Your mother?"

"She died," Alexander trailed off.

"Oh, I'm sorry to hear that," she allowed a moment of silence. "I haven't spoken with my parents in years. Eight, to be exact."

"Maybe it's time."

"There are too many memories there. Reminders of what I should have been."

"You're never going to see them again?"

"I never said that. Like all people, I'm sure if there's a death in the family, or even a near-death, I'll swallow my pride. Death's the supreme perspective maker."

Alexander did not respond.

"Have you painted anything recently?" she said.

"The last thing I did was right before she died. I haven't been able to pick up a paintbrush since."

Her eyes widened, sympathy and pity entered her voice, "How sad. What type of things *did* you paint?"

"Homelessness, sickness, women living on the streets with their children, fallen birds on the brink of death, senseless violence, everlasting love, people being used. Mainly things I saw which made me feel something more than numbness. I didn't keep any of them though. I got rid of them along with everything else from my past."

"You didn't keep anything?"

"Only a charcoal drawing of my mother . . . when she was dying. I couldn't use color anymore."

"How did she die?"

"Her heart stopped beating."

"Undeniably," snapped Angela. "How old were you?"

"Eighteen."

"What did you do with the drawing?"

"I'm not really sure."

She knew he was lying.

"Oh, that's a shame. I really would like to have seen it."

"It's nothing special, just death on paper."

Angela did not respond. Alexander's eyes drained, the blue turning to a dull grey. In a twisted way, Angela felt special she was able to arouse such an emotion in him; it gave her sick satisfaction. She shifted in her seat, feeling the warmth rise from her thighs to her brain. She knew the situation was conquered. Alexander was putty in her hands. With a smile, she leaned across the table and whispered the only thing which seemed suitable. "Can we go back to your place?"

Alexander's eyes glazed.

Frozen air passes through the forest. Only ambitious animals make noises in the dark. The trees are particularly green, their presence known only by the clicking of pine needles. Asphalt cuts through the nature, snow hesitantly hugging its edges.

The road is silent.

A wooden sign stands on the side of the street with snow covering the words. Below it, a dirt road melts into the forest. The air stirs again, awaking the demons of the trees. They snicker through the night about stories of the past.

Angela left before the sun. It had been two hours since Alexander turned away from her, hoping she would think he was asleep. She knew he was awake, wanting her to leave. The actions which had taken place during the evening had left her with an unusual feeling teetering between emptiness and grim satisfaction. She had been with numerous indifferent men during sex. Alexander was different. He performed the textbook actions with no passion. She felt his frigidity. Visions of the drawing of his mother poured into her mind with Alexander's lifeless body in his mother's place. He was alive with an aura of emptiness.

He might as well have been dead.

During the hours Alexander lay awake, Angela looked at him, hoping for a response. Time passed. No words. She haphazardly left, purposely leaving her panties on the pillow. An old habit, regardless of the night's outcome. The distance from Alexander's apartment to her car was an eternity. She fiddled for the keys in her purse as the sunrise poured into her eyes.

She stood statuesque as a man in neon green shorts approached, a Pomeranian on a pink leash with a diamond-studded collar at his side. "You all right, sweetie," he lisped.

Angela shook her head, "Just leaving a friend's house."

He looked at her strewn hair, no make-up and lack of a panty line, "I've had my share of late night 'friends' also." He shot a glance at the apartment complex, "It wasn't Ricky, was it? That bitch never can decide what team he's playing for. Oh, but with those pecks and his ..." he trailed off, "Anyway, you've experienced it deeply..."

"It wasn't Ricky."

"I see..."

The dog barked. "Hush Liza," he spat. "Are you sure you'll be okay? When a person leaves so early..."

"On the contrary, I think he saved my life."

"I feel a coldness through my body when I'm next to anything living. I get uncomfortable and tense and question everything."

Alexander sat in a chair next to Truman's Christmas tree.

"Angela quit today. Kristin said she went back home to her parents . . . I talked about my mother last night. I really didn't want to bring her up. It just came out. As the words drifted into the air, I knew any chance with her was over. For some reason though, she didn't leave, she wanted to go back to my place. After ... no, I should probably say during, there was a look on her face . . . it was like all the others, when they feel what I feel. I saw the moment the numbness reached her brain. She looked like she wanted to scream."

He clenched his teeth. "I want this hatred to end. I want to feel the way I did before, to be able to not only see colors like those outside the window, but also create them. You're the lucky one, you know. At least sometimes I think the patients here are lucky. At least more than most people, because the only loss they experience is of themselves. Not of their children, their parents, or even their dogs. I told Angela last night the only innocent people are the unconscious and young children. I suppose many could argue they're one in the same, but I disagree. Maybe that's why I spend most of my time with both, to get the better of each world.

"Hearing all this, you probably wouldn't believe I head a youth program. Did I ever tell you about it? To quote the pamphlet, it's an

'Organization which helps the underprivileged have a place for refuge'. A lot of its just activities like sports and community projects, but it keeps the kids off the streets.

"Of course, I'm not to be excluded in the masses when it comes to vindictive thoughts and actions. Once, a few years ago, one of my friends told me about a medical project he was working on. He spewed his aspirations and goals, of all the things I used to believe in when I was young. As he talked, he had the same passion I did about art. He went on for hours, telling me his theories and studies. I sat and listened, even offered occasional reassurance. Deep down, however, I felt relentless jealousy. I wanted him to fail...

"I didn't see him again until a few weeks ago and before he spoke I knew my wish came true. His eyes had an emptiness which most people in this world possess. After he told me his tale of discontent, I left with a sense of satisfaction. When I got home it transformed into sickness. It overtook my body like an unrelenting monster. I could not fathom how I wanted a close friend to fail. I hovered over the toilet, trying to release my jealously and contempt through vomit.

"That night I realized there's something in everyone which makes them vindictive. I don't consider myself a spiteful or hateful person. Nonetheless, it overcame me. It took a while for me to realize this was not a downfall of my abilities as a person, but as a human. I believe it is the nature of us all to only want what is best for ourselves and only ourselves. When we see someone else accomplishing the voids of our lives, contempt encompasses the situation.

"That's why everyone says forgiveness is the supreme action in life. I remember as a child always hearing, 'You need to forgive'. Unfortunately, forgiveness is a very strong word to comply with."

Alexander woke with a jolt, sweat streaming from his forehead. Eyes slits, he unconsciously grabbed for the clock and held it an inch from his face. The blaring, red, digital numbers bore 11:45 p.m. He stayed sitting, falling asleep, clock in hand. He woke like every other morning, sheets strewn across the bed and clock on the table.

He did not remember waking during the night.

The trees stirred outside the hospital window, making it impossible to hear the ticking of the clock. As the hand reached the forty-fifth minute of the eleventh hour, Truman's eyes fluttered open. The moonlight from the window pierced his brain. He slowly looked across the room. He tried to speak and move but neither abided. He lay still as his eyes slowly drooped, taking him back to the world of his unconscious mind.

The high-pitched ring echoed through Alexander's brain. With his head still in a pillow, he reached over, shoving the phone off the table.

"Shit" muffled beneath the down feathers.

He slowly sat upright as "Hello?" repeatedly came from the receiver. He rubbed his hands over his face, working blood through his pin-pricked muscles.

He picked up the phone and said groggily, "Hello?"

"Alexander, is that you?"

"Yeah. Who is this?"

"It's Kristin, from work."

Alexander sighed, "It's my day off, what do you want?"

He rubbed his face with his left hand, cradling the receiver.

"He woke up."

Alexander's hand froze.

He slowly pulled it from his face.

"Who?"

"Truman…Ah, Truman Cooper."

"When did it happen?"

"We're not really sure, but when the doctor went into his room this morning, his eyes were open and he was mumbling soft words."

"What was he saying?"

"I'm not sure. They don't tell me much around here."

"Never mind. I'll be right down."

Alexander knew word of the waking spread. When he walked into Truman's room, all of the doctors were present. Jeffery, Dr. Saxon, and Dr. Barrett were vultures at the foot of the bed. They all smiled, pretending to be friends, even though detestation lingered.

Truman was wide-eyed and sitting upright. Alexander cautiously motioned toward him. Dr. Saxon quickly interrupted his path, "Alexander! How are you doing my boy? I see you've heard the news," his smile widened. "Kristin can't keep a secret on her life, can she?"

He put his arm around Alexander's neck, hand upon his shoulder. Alexander looked at the pudgy digits resting upon him. He smiled in disgust. The rest of the doctors paid no attention, each too busy with self-congratulations. He was certain they already argued who was the greatest influence to Truman's recovery, even though they scarcely knew his name. Alexander envisioned each of them waking to the ringing phone – *Hello? Cooper who? Don't you know I need sleep...oh...awake? I'll be right there.*

"I don't think you've been properly introduced," said Dr. Saxon. "Alexander Douglas, meet Truman Cooper."

There was a long silence.

Alexander wanted to know what Truman was thinking.

Truman slowly slurred, "Roooose."

Jeffery clapped. "Rose! Excellent! The more you speak, the quicker you'll recover. You have to remember it's been over a year since you've said anything; not to mention, your jaw was pretty smashed up after that beating."

Truman's eyes widened. Alexander could tell Truman had no memory of the attack. He quietly sighed.

Jeffery noticed Truman's surprise and quickly said, "Yes, well," he looked toward the other doctors, "Gentlemen, shall we?"

They nodded in agreement and scurried to the door.

"Congratulations, Truman," Jeffrey said as he gazed at the ceiling. "Someone must've been looking over you."

He looked at Alexander, "Feel free to ask Alexander any questions. Otherwise, I'll be back later to run some tests. Make sure all the bells and whistles are working."

He slithered out the door before anyone could respond.

Alexander and Truman looked at each other.

Words were not exchanged.

Alexander sat down in the chair next to the tree. He immediately noticed the tree's browning needles but pushed the thought from his mind. He leaned back, crossed his legs, and motioned to talk but stopped as he saw Truman's helplessness, confusion, and fear all wrapped in a blank stare.

"You've been given a great gift," started Alexander. "Of course, some might say it's a great burden."

He was about to continue the monologue when he realized Truman had not moved any part of his body. Horror ran through him as he thought of his selfish act of human redemption when there was a bigger threat of Truman's paralyzation.

"Are you able to move?"

Truman wiggled his toes.

"Do you remember anything?"

Truman licked his quivering lips.

Words did not leave his tongue.

Alexander nodded.

Truman helplessly watched as Alexander exited the room. He returned with a small item.

"I borrowed this from Kristin," Alexander said.

He lifted a mirror. Truman's eyes widened as Alexander approached.

"We might as well get the hard part over with."

Truman watched his face pour into the mirror. He moved his head slowly from side to side. There were two jagged, pinkish scars, resembling puffed marshmallows. The larger ran from his scalp to his right eyebrow, the smaller across his left cheek. As Truman gazed into the mirror, slowly running his fingers over his face, Alexander talked to him about past happenings. He explained where the paramedics found him, his injuries, and how long he had been unconscious.

"You always said Mommy."

Truman looked up from the mirror, eyes blank.

"We tried to find her, even though we only had your license to go off of, but we didn't have any luck. You don't remember her, do you? It was the only word you muttered the past year or so; they told me you even said it in the ambulance. Of course, I wasn't there during the initial stuff. I only deal with them after the blood is washed away."

At the apprehension of the doctors, Alexander took Truman out of the hospital a few days after he woke. Legs motionless and atrophied, Truman was far from walking on his own, so Alexander took him by wheelchair. Truman grimaced as Alexander shifted his body. He was pushed outside, to the rows of green trees puncturing the clouds above.

Truman's face eased. "My dream."

"What did you say?"

Truman did not respond.

Alexander grunted as he pushed Truman onto the bumpy grass and into the forest. The sunlight was minimal amongst the trees, revealing itself through cracks in the branches. Alexander took a deep breath.

"Take that in, Truman. It's been a while since you've smelt anything but puke and piss."

Truman's chest heaved as he breathed as heavily as his muscles allowed.

"I know you're probably frustrated, but the speech therapist will start your treatments this week. We'll get your muscles back in working order. You'll be running around in no time."

They sat silently amongst the trees, listening to the awakened wind.

Alexander walked into Truman's room and found the speech therapist on the ground, on all fours, picking up scattered cards containing various images with their corresponding name beneath in bold black letters:

CAT

BASEBALL

He watched as the therapist finished stacking the cards, quietly putting them in a plastic bag at her side. Truman was propped in his bed, eyes red and slightly puffy. Tears had already been wiped away.

"Hello?"

"Oh, hello Alexander," she said.

She was a heavyset woman in her early forties whose attitude pushed annoyance.

"How's everything going?" asked Alexander.

Truman turned his head toward the window.

When the therapist saw Truman was looking away, she quickly turned to Alexander and motioned to exit. He followed her out the door.

"He's having a little difficulty," she whispered.

Alexander tried to keep a straight face but was unable to rid the thoughts of her, hunched over like an elephant, picking up the strewn cards. He bit the inside of his cheek, refraining a laugh, and spat, "I noticed."

She looked at the bag of cards, "It's very common for a person in his condition to be frustrated. He's having to learn things all over again. Don't get me wrong, he's making great progress but he's easily flustered. There's been some difficulty with a few simple words, like 'heaven' which caused . . ." she raised the crinkled bag, "well, you know the rest."

Alexander looked at the bag and had no doubt she got the flash cards at some Christian thrift store. He tried to think what children's picture was used for the depiction of heaven.

The therapist's glasses slipped to the edge of her nose; she pushed them back with her link sausage finger. "I just want everyone to give him the support he needs during this trying time. I hope once he gets over the initial hump, sentences and conjugations will flow with ease."

"What about his memories? Will this help trigger anything ?"

She shrugged, "That's a little out of my league. I just help them start talking. I'm used to working with children, Mr. Douglas, and with children, lack of memory usually isn't an issue." She smiled, "Then again, Mr. Cooper's reaction was not far off from the three-year-olds I deal with."

She did not wait for a goodbye from Alexander. "I will see him again in two days."

Alexander poked his head around the corner and found Truman looking out the window, a motionless statue. He quietly walked over and sat down. He looked at the empty space next to him where the tree previously resided. When it was finally removed, it had been days since it was watered. The excitement of Truman's waking pushed simple things into the background; he also had to throw away a wilted fern from room fifteen. A portion of the tree's needles fell to the ground, leaving a trail down the hall, to the trash.

Alexander saw a few brown needles he missed. He picked them up and scoured for twigs hidden in the tile pattern.

"Rough morning?"

He remained bent over but turned his head toward Truman who looked back at him. Tears streamed down his cheeks.

Alexander grunted as he rose.

"I don't think anyone said it was going to be easy. It's a miracle you're even awake, or alive for that matter, and to ask yourself to be back to full capacity so soon is unrealistic."

He patted Truman's knee, "Give it time."

His words comforted Truman who looked out the window as the rain began to pour.

"Absolutely wonderful."

Truman smiled at the complement.

"I'm serious, Truman. I'm amazed you've rebounded so quickly," said Alexander. "Can you believe it's only been a few months since you stopped the therapy? Read it one more time aloud?"

Truman picked up the worn copy of Dr. Seuss' *And To Think That I Saw It On Mulberry Street*. Alexander brought it in, a favorite from his childhood. He watched Truman read the book without complications.

"What do you think the book is about?" asked Alexander.

"Telling lies?"

"No. Look deeper. Read the last page again."

Truman looked up from the book, his face blank.

"Well?" asked Alexander.

Alexander turned the page back.

"Look here, where the dad asks him if anything excited him. The boy has an entire story conjured up but he resolves to telling the simplest version. The dull version. The entire book is a testament to imagination.

On the surface, you may think it's about a young boy who tells lies, but I think it shows the imagination of children being suppressed by parents. The ending suffices both groups of people - those who always want there to be logic and answers in life, and those who see everything on the grandest scale. The father thinks the boy has grown-up and rid himself of ridiculous exaggerations, yet, in reality, the boy is humoring him. He continues to have wonderful stories inside. Stories to share with those people who want to hear them. Anyway, just realize the surface of most stories don't have the greater meaning. You have to dig a little. Find the truth in it."

"I'll try."

"Wonderful! Now, since you've made such great progress with your speech, are you up to trying your movements again?"

Truman's color drained.

"Truman, you know you don't want to stay in that wheelchair forever."

"I know. I'm just – "

"Scared? It's all right to be scared. I'm sure the scariest thing is thinking you may not be able to walk again, and you probably don't want to try because you don't want to find out the truth."

Truman looked down at his feet, "Can we wait until tomorrow for the disappointment?"

"Very good," said Alexander confidently.

Truman grunted as he moved the walker a few inches ahead. His arms bulged as his feet pulled forward, scratching along the linoleum.

"Excellent," said Alexander.

Truman strained a smile. Sweat poured from his head into a pool on the floor.

He slowly circled the room.

"Truman, watch out for your sweat– "

Truman's legs came under him.

Snap.

He lay on the ground, a pretzel, his feet tangled beneath his body, right wrist joint as large as a golf ball.

Alexander kneeled, "Shit. Are you all right? Can you feel this?"

He gently pressed on the bulge.

"Fuck," clenched Truman as a tear streamed down his cheek.

A small drop of blood ran from his lower lip as he pried away his teeth.

"You broke it," said Alexander.

"No shit."

Truman licked away the blood and moaned as he pulled himself to a sitting position. His pants smelled of sweat, which left a piss-looking stain wrapping from his anus to genitals.

"Why the fuck didn't they just let me die?" he gasped.

Alexander pushed the walker aside and picked Truman off the floor, "Because I wouldn't let them."

In an effort to resolve some of Truman's endless questions of his past, Alexander brought him the bags of items from his old apartment, previously stowed away in the basement of the hospital.

In searching, Alexander filtered through some of the other patients' items, throwing most of the unmarked, dust-ridden boxes aside.

"Gail Summer," he said softly.

A patient in her early eighties with no family or visitors. She's nearing the end, thought Alexander.

He ran his fingers over her name; the white chalk soaked into his fingertips. Like Gail, the scrawls had faded with age. At the top of the overflowing items was a small music box. He picked it up carefully, quickly noticing a piece of paper taped to the back. He read it aloud: "Hold for Jennifer Schwartz."

Alexander looked at the paper in appal. Jennifer was one of the doctor's assistants. She rummaged through the belongings of each patient, thought Alexander, trying to find personal treasures. Sickness rose in his stomach as he pictured Jennifer waiting for Gail to die. He crumpled the piece of paper and threw it aside. It rolled into a corner, not to be discovered for years.

He fell to the ground, hands and body trembling, and covered his face. Thin drool and tears ran to the floor as he cradled the box.

❧

Alexander roamed the emergency room halls, a small plastic bag at his side. Although he did not work in the hospital, he visited enough for some of the nurses to know him by name, the lucky ones knowing him by size and shape. Or more specifically, deep and wide. Shirley Slater's eyes wandered to his jeans as he passed, a motion he usually entertained but this evening ignored. He scurried through the corridors until he noticed a room with an ajar door. Inside was a young girl, no older than thirteen, sitting next to a bed.

In the bed laid a sleeping early-thirties female. Mother, thought Alexander. Bingo.

Alexander quietly entered, "Hello?"

The girl looked over at him. The woman in the bed had abrasions across her face and her left leg was elevated, in a cast.

"Hello," responded the girl, "Are you one of the doctors?"

"No. I'm actually, I'm a nurse."

The young girl shook her head in approval.

"What's your name?" asked Alexander.

"Stephanie."

Alexander looked over at her mother, "What happened to your mother?"

She hesitantly responded, "She was in a car accident a couple of days ago. They said she has mild swelling around her brain."

Alexander shook his head in understanding. He walked closer. "I was wondering if you could do something for me?"

"That depends ..."

"Safe answer."

He pulled the music box from the bag.

Stephanie's eyes lit up.

"I'm caring for an elderly woman who has no friends and family. She wanted to give this to someone deserving."

"I can't take that." She looked over at her mom. "What would I tell her?"

Alexander placed the box in her lap. "Tell her a generous old woman gave it to you. Tell her it was from Gail Summer."

Truman and Alexander were curious of the cigarette smell. Truman rummaged through each bag slowly, mainly consisting of clothing. He examined each item, trying to remember. Alexander remained the entire time, watching the process with curiosity. Truman's final disillusionment at lack of remembrance did not appear to affect him.

Alexander placed the black trash bags on the ground as he and Truman entered the dark room. Two large, black teardrops. Truman walked slowly behind, his cane clicking on the ground in unison with deep breaths.

Alexander turned the light on, revealing a small room connecting to an even smaller kitchen. Carpet to linoleum. There was a small stove, microwave, and refrigerator; other modern luxuries were not to be found.

Alexander clasped his hands together, "Well, this is the happy home. Unfortunately, all I have to offer is a couch, there's only one bedroom in this five star resort."

"It's safe to expect a buffet in the morning?"

"Only if you drag your ass out of bed and make the food yourself."

He led Truman down a short hallway to a bathroom. To the right was an ajar door. Inside, the bed almost encompassed the entire room.

"There's a towel for you above the shitter," Alexander walked into his room. "I cleared out the bottom drawers in my dresser. You'll probably have to live out of your bags for the most part. Make yourself at home. I set it up for you to meet Julianne tomorrow. I put in the good word so she should give you some type of job."

"Thanks for everything."

He shrugged indifferently, "I have to keep an eye on you, I have a lot of time invested."

Alexander cooked as Truman slowly made his way into the bedroom, his cane in one hand, articles of clothing in the other. *Thump. Thump.* Truman opened the top drawer, forgetting Alexander had cleared the bottom two. As he shut it, a paper caught his eye. He reopened it slowly, revealing a small charcoal drawing of a dead body upon roses. It was simple but the contrast of black and white shot fiercely into his mind.

Alexander's footsteps approached.

Truman quickly shut the drawer, closing the possibility of answers to lingering questions.

Julianne sat silently in her chair, eyes filled with doubt. She leaned into Truman folding her hands on top of the desk.

"I'll be honest with you. I'm not real keen on the idea of hiring someone without having some background check."

Julianne's sharp features fit her persona, her pointy nose was especially upsetting to Truman.

"Well, I'm not so sure about my background either," Truman quietly interjected, "or my name for that matter."

She waved the response off as she leaned back, "Yes, yes, Alexander told me all about what happened to you. Tragic, just tragic," there was no sympathy in her tone, "But I'm trying to run a clean place here, got it? I don't want any of those guys coming in here to start trouble, do you understand?"

"I'm sorry, are you mistaking me for someone else?"

"Excuse me?"

He repeated himself, drawling out each word.

"I'm not sure what you mean– "

"I guess I'm just confused. If Alexander told you what had happened, you would surely know I don't remember who did this," he pointed to his scar, "to me."

Julianne cracked her neck in unease. Truman was satisfied with her flush face and was certain she slightly gagged.

"Keep in mind, I'm only doing this as a favor to Alexander. He's done a lot to help out around here. However, you need to understand that even with his good word on you, if you step out of line, that's it. These kids come here to get away from turmoil, not to find it."

She swiftly got out of her chair and was at the office door in one glorious sweep. She opened it before Truman realized the conversation was over.

She turned to him with a degree of annoyance. "So, are you coming? I'd like to show you around and let you meet some of the regulars."

He obeyed, following her around the center, initially making sure to lag a few feet behind. He then walked a half step in front of her. She shot a challenging glance, prompting him to move back.

She pointed to different boys and girls, relaying names as they passed. He gave each a slight nod and handshake. They walked through the game room and gym, where most of the socializing took place, then into the library.

Julianne whispered, "We have quite a collection here. Mostly donated books. A great selection of the classics. Do you read the classics, Mr. Cooper?"

"I'm fond of the Marquis de Sade."

Julianne turned her back. "I'm not sure if this is going to work, Mr. Cooper."

"Please," he implored, "call me Truman."

A chuckle surfaced from the far corner where a teenage boy hunched over a book. He briefly looked up, giving Truman an honorable smile.

"Who's that?"

Julianne reluctantly answered, "Jason. Mr. Cooper, as I was saying —"

Truman violently waved off her words as walked toward Jason.

"You're wasting your time Mr. Cooper. He won't talk to you."

Truman ignored her.

"Eavesdropping can be a socially unacceptable habit," said Truman.

"Like interrupting a person who's reading?" responded Jason.

Jason looked up from the pages.

"Touche," said Truman. "What do you think?"

"About what?"

"My conversation with the woman who has never been told 'no'."

Jason looked past Truman to Julianne, who was waiting by the door impatiently.

"You mean Ms. Personality?"

"What are you reading?"

"*The Kreutzer Sonata.*"

"Is it any good?"

Jason shrugged.

"Not sure if I've read that one, why did you choose that book?" Truman said.

"It's for school," he hesitated then looked at Truman with a curious glance, "What do you mean, 'Not sure'?"

"I don't remember much. My memory is a little spaced."

"You're shitting me right? So what happened to you?"

Truman looked into his eyes, "How old are you?"

"Fifteen."

"You look older."

"A drunk mom and abusive dad will do that to a person. What's it to you what I've been through?"

"Not much actually, I was just curious."

"What about you?"

"You tell me."

Jason probed his eyes; his face slowly changed from unconvinced and stern to soft.

"That bad?" asked Truman.

"No, just lost."

"Okay, I think we need to move on, Mr. Cooper," said Julianne.

Jason's final word drowned beneath her overpowering tone. Julianne looked into Jason's eyes, seeing responsiveness in his persona for the first time. She slowly backed away for lack of a better reaction.

"Well, I guess you both have some things to talk about," she paused. "Let me know if you need anything."

Julianne left.

Jason and Truman looked at each other in silence, which Jason broke first.

Over an hour passed before Truman returned to Julianne's office. Her face was flush, sweat beads on her brow, possibly from pacing the room, Truman thought. She wants to pick my brain. The blinds were drawn. He assumed she did not want to have the teenagers looking in on her anticipation. She guided him by the arm to the seat; her grip was light, not fierce like he would have expected.

Her voice was not one of condemnation, but instead of curiosity. "I've never seen anything like it."

"What do you mean?"

"Jason has never opened up to anyone. What did he say?" She shook her head, "No, no … that's between you and him. I only want you to tell me if there's a threat to his safety."

Truman smiled at her refrain. "Well, he's definitely had it tough. He's just cautious but not necessarily antisocial. With a little urging from the right people he could be a good source of knowledge for some of these kids."

Julianne clapped her hands together.

"Can you start tomorrow? You can come in the same time as Alexander."

- - -

The following weeks were a combination of meetings and relationship building. Julianne gave the introductions, Truman told his story. Each were like campfire meetings, wide-eyed children grasping every word, mesmerized, no longer caring about smores or venomous snakes hidden in the bushes. His speeches gave the children a different perspective on situations they thought they had no control over: abuse, abandonment, drugs.

As Truman became an intricate part of the center, Jason ventured from the confines of the library to speak with him; it often turned into conversing with other teenagers. As Jason broke from his mold, Truman had a gratification he had not felt since he regained consciousness. He found more happiness in supporting the troubled kids than when he regained his abilities to walk and speak. With this realization, he knew helping people would be the only thing to replenish his undetermined emptiness.

Kim

"Then he saw perfection."

Alexander looked up from his book, "What?"

Truman did not answer. He sat mesmerized, his eyelids not taking the time to blink. Alexander followed Truman's path of sight, falling upon a young girl of about eighteen or nineteen.

Truman looked at her, eyes glazed, mouth slightly ajar, "Indescribable lust. She enters an unknown vestibule filled with unfamiliar faces. She is reluctant to approach, " he paused admiring her as she stood motionless in the doorway, "I must talk to her."

"The subject of such a climactic meeting?"

"Anything she wants."

"If she wanted to talk about bowel movements and urinary discharge you would just stand there complacently nodding like cupid just shot you in the ass?"

Truman's face was stern.

Alexander chuckled. His smile turned to a frown as he saw Truman's mouth prune and eyes narrow. He placed the book on the table and sat upright, looking at the young girl, this time with vested interest, then back at Truman's unfaltering face.

"You're serious about talking to her, aren't you?"

Words were distant. Truman heard light footsteps as she approached. In her eyes he saw understanding and compassion, two things he had not previously seen in a woman. He was entranced with her brown eyes; they were too dark to separate the iris from the pupil, each melding into each other, to his pure satisfaction.

She was halfway across the room when Truman was able to focus on other features. Her complexion was dark, hair pulled back in a ponytail, laying just above the ears. A strand had somehow freed itself from the rest of the mass and curved down her cheekbone. It slightly moved with each step. He wanted to push the fallen strand behind her ear, only to have an excuse to touch her. The girl was wearing simple shoes and an unrevealing black dress, although he could tell there were beautiful curves hidden beneath. Her choice of apparel would likely divert eyes than draw looks. Truman felt this was the purpose of the dress but he could not figure why.

The young girl looked nervously over her shoulder, at the exit, prepared to bolt at the slightest uncomfortable feeling. Truman saw the reasoning of her concealment. On the girl's previously unseen cheek, there was a large bruise, extending from ear to chin. Truman's face twitched as he vicariously felt the slap.

He could tell she had not been scarce to beatings, knowing that if her cheek were a one-time occurrence, her hair would have been down, trying to cover the mark. She did not even apply make-up to the area. She no longer cared who knew what was happening to her.

As she passed children involved in table tennis and billiards, each raised their heads, drawn to her. When they saw abuse, they returned to their games. Her face was an unwanted reminder of past bruises.

Truman stood in front of the table as she approached.

She nervously fidgeted her fingers.

Her voice was quiet. "I was wondering if you could help me."

Alexander sat and watched the exchange with anticipation. It was the first time Truman had walked without his cane.

Truman did not know what to tell the girl, the uncomfortable swell in his stomach taking hold. He reached his right hand out, raising it to her head. She stiffened, waiting for it to come across her face with force. He gently ran his fingers over the bruise, then stuck his neck out slightly kissing her cheek.

Alexander and the surrounding children became wide-eyed.

Truman brought his head back; the girl was crying.

Truman fell vulnerably into her pupils. Extended, uncomfortable silence. Everything froze. He looked to Alexander for help, who only looked at him and the girl, into them. Words would not pass Truman's lips, so he gently raised her hand, which was dry from the cold air, and kissed the top of it.

Victoria.

She was looking for refuge from her past, from her boyfriend Vincent, who was deeper in the bottle than a worm in tequila. She was the main recipient of his rage for the greater part of their three-year relationship. Her mother died when she was twelve and her father was an empty shell:

present in body but lacking in mind, the latter dying with her mother. Victoria walked into his bedroom soon after her death and found him cradling her mother's undergarments, slowly caressing them between his thumb and finger in a continuous, circular motion.

He was no help when Victoria was scared.

She looked in each corner and shadow she passed, knowing Vincent was not far behind.

She stumbled through the explanation.

Julianne overheard the conversation and rushed out of her office. She placed her arm around Victoria, shielding her from the travesties of Truman and Alexander. Shielding her from men.

Julianne stood, telephone in hand, barking orders into the receiver. Victoria sat calmly, her back to the office window. As Julianne spoke, she watched Truman outside her office, sitting at his desk, staring at the back of Victoria's head, his jaw slightly agape.

She slammed the phone down and forced a smile, "There's a shelter down the street that you'll be able to stay at for the time being. I'll take you there in a couple of hours."

She looked past Victoria, to Truman's gawking face, "I'm sorry if those guys did anything to offend you. They mean well."

Julianne shrugged as she walked behind her desk, putting both hands on the desktop, leaning into it. "I'll make sure you're taken care of."

She wrote on a small tablet of paper and handed it to Victoria, "If anything is unsatisfactory, this is my home number. You can call me at any hour."

Victoria took the paper, held it with both hands, her knuckles turning white.

I was wondering if you could help me.

Victoria's words echoed through Truman's head for weeks. He stood outside the shelter, in the cold, pelting rain, mumbling continuous words as passers looked askew.

Words.

Their strength is unexplainable, thought Truman. They can be spoken, yelled, whispered, shrieked, panted, in moments of climax.

"I was wondering if you could help me," he said for the first time.

He stood silent, allowing the rain to flow down his cheeks. He took a half step toward the door, stopped, grabbed the handle and slowly pulled, holding it ajar, deliberating.

"Can you please shut that? I don't need water all over the place," said a shrill voice from inside.

Truman obeyed.

Approximately fifteen feet away was a counter top with a floating head. He could not see the body hidden below, and judging from the face, he did not care to. It was unforgiving. She appeared to Truman a seventy-five-year-old in a thirty-year-old body, her contempt for life eating away at her years prematurely, leaving the devastated remains. Her hair was pulled up, away from her face, although he wished it wasn't. Her naturally condescending nose pointed up, her crow's feet predominant and wrinkles violently scattered across her cheeks and forehead .

"Can I help you?" The shrillness did not subside.

Truman made motion to approach, "Uh…"

"Wipe your shoes."

He stopped abruptly, almost falling on his face. He looked down at his feet, seeing a tattered towel. He started to wipe. The woman rose from behind the counter and watched.

"Yes. That'll do."

When Truman looked up, he had a small smile, which quickly dissipated, seeing her frown.

"Can I help you?"

"I'm here to see someone," said Truman meekly.

Her posture straightened. "I'm sure you are."

"Oh no, it's not like that," he said.

She was unconvinced.

"I'm here to see Victoria…"

He did not know her last name.

"She's got dark hair," he used his hands as he spoke, trying to mold a picture. He ran his finger along his cheek, "She had a bruise right here when she came to you a couple of weeks ago."

Although he did not think it possible, the woman's posture stiffened further.

"We do not allow visitors unless you're on our list. And you're not on our list."

He sighed, "Please. Just talk with her, let her know I'm here. I can't stop thinking about her."

"It's very unorthodox…"

"Just tell her who I am. If she says she doesn't want to see me, I'll leave, no questions asked."

"Well, what's your name?"

"She wouldn't know that. Just tell her," he paused, "her hands could use lotion."

Victoria reluctantly poked her head around the corner. When she saw Truman, the corners of her mouth turned up slightly, but only briefly. She revealed the rest of her body and slowly approached. The woman behind the counter followed Victoria's few steps.

"It's all right Kim," said Victoria.

Kim shook her head in approval and returned to her seat, eyes not leaving Truman.

"I wanted to give a proper introduction," he held out his hand, "I'm Truman Cooper."

Victoria accepted his outstretched hand with a black leather glove, "Victoria Demme, and your initial introduction is more than satisfactory."

Truman looked outside at the rain, which had slowed to a drizzle. "Would you be able to go on a quick walk?"

She looked over his shoulder, out the window, "In the rain?"

"Through hail, through sleet, through snow."

"Just like the postal service? Such dedication. All right, let's go."

Kim's mouth clenched in disapproval. "Ten minutes."

Victoria shook her head in agreement; Truman already opened the door; water streamed onto the doormat. Kim looked at him scornfully.

They strolled down the street in silence as droplets fell upon their cheeks.

"I see your bruise is gone."

Victoria subconsciously felt her cheek, "Yeah, they usually don't stay long."

"This has happened before?"

She looked down to the gutter at the water flowing rapidly toward a storm drain.

"Sorry. I didn't mean to upset you."

"It's not your fault. You didn't hit me."

"Yeah, but I know how you feel."

She looked up at him with half-curiosity and half-disdain.

In an attempt to clear the air of doubt, he told his story.

With his conclusion her face turned apologetic.

"You have no family or friends?" asked Victoria.

"No one for reunions or large, glad-handed barbeques."

"And you don't remember anything about the assault?"

"Their shoes. Brown and black. The black ones were slick; I remember seeing my face in them as they struck."

Ahead a large puddle hugged the sidewalk.

"I should probably get back," said Victoria, "I don't want Kim to call the authorities."

"No, I wouldn't want to feel her wrath."

"Men," she smiled, "are not highly regarded where I'm at."

"First we need to do something."

"What?"

He motioned to the water. She looked over and smiled. He held his hand out to her.

Victoria laughed as they landed. Standing ankle-deep in gasoline-saturated water, a pain shot through Truman's skull.

His grip tightened.

"Ouch!" she pulled her hand back, shaking it limply. "What was that for?"

He leaned over and spat blood into the water.

"Oh my God, are you all right?"

"Yeah. I get rushes of pain in my head, then blood, always a mouthful of it. Warm and salty bitterness."

He put his hand to his head, rubbing it slowly with his eyes shut.

"My God," Victoria touched his hand, "Is that from..."

He opened his eyes, "What's that? Oh, yeah, it's one of them."

Truman parted his hair, revealing a scar which started above his ear and spanned to the back of his head.

"Not too appetizing, huh? It takes a little while to get used to. When I first looked at it, picturing my head smashed open, gore and grey matter seeping down my face, a shiver ran up my spine...do you want to touch it?"

"That's probably the last thing I want to do."

"Your choice, but it probably won't look so bad after you feel it."

"And what makes you think that?"

"Have you ever seen a horror movie? It's like those scenes where the girl is gutted and left to die, the first time you see it you may be a little disgusted, but after a few views, it's not so upsetting, like you've become desensitized."

"Interesting analogy. Not very appealing, but interesting," Victoria started to lift her shirt, "Okay, I'll touch it only if you touch this."

She revealed a jagged scar on her right side, just below her hip.

"Vincent's car keys," she rhythmically caressed the area, eyes shut, "This is what I got for asking him to stop drinking."

Truman placed his fingers on top of hers, running along the scar. He felt it curiously as she put her free hand under his hair, feeling the smooth strip of skin on his head. She lightly moaned as he caressed. She imagined the stitches wrapping around his head as he imagined Vincent's keys splitting her side.

"What do you want me to do with those?"

"Take them," replied Victoria.

Reluctantly, Truman took the binoculars. "Okay, now what?"

She pointed in the distance, to a house on a hill. "Look in there, the second window to the left."

"What am I looking at?"

"Don't you see her? In the chair?"

"No..." Truman's eyes adjusted and focused, "Wait. I see something. It looks like an old woman. I can only see her head though, it's moving back and forth."

"She's rocking."

"What's so special about a lady rocking?"

"That's all she ever does. Rocking. Morning and night. I know because I used to come here a lot and watch her. It's quite soothing. She was my reminder."

"Of what?"

"That one day I would be like her if I stayed with Vincent. A vegetable. I looked her up, she's just another sad case of abuse. One of the names of women on a never-ending list." Victoria paused. "She was the only consistent thing in my life, she's what finally prompted me to take action. I know it may not be much, but I wanted to show her to you because I think you're the only one who can understand her importance. You and I one in the same you know, cheaters of death. We've both seen the face of fear and destruction, just like this woman, but the difference is that we survived."

"Since you showed me your place of solace, I thought I would do the same."

Victoria looked in awe at the towering trees.

"I come here a lot, especially at night, when the wind howls and the moon shatters the branches," said Truman. "When I was asleep I only dreamed of tranquil places. The main dream was of a mass of trees and a dirt road running through it. Someday I'll find that road and see where it leads. The unconscious. I can guarantee all's not well in their mind. My thoughts were in constant turmoil, but I knew I could do nothing about it."

"What troubled you?"

"I'm not sure. There were constant, disturbing images. I only completely remember things of nature. Snow layered trees, frozen winds– ."

"Inconspicuous dirt roads?"

"Something like that. There was a sign too."

"What did it say?"

"It was covered with snow."

She laughed, "A dirt road and a snow-covered sign?"

"Yeah," he smiled, " I guess I'll have to be content with these trees."

It was one of the few weeks that rain had not poured. Truman laid upon his back, looking to the sky. Victoria followed his lead.

"I could stay here forever, amongst the trees," said Victoria.

"Yeah, it definitely wouldn't be a bad final resting spot. I've always liked the smell of pine needles."

Truman rolled on his side, looking at Victoria. She noticed his gaze after a few moments and rolled the opposite way in embarrassment.

"Don't turn away..."

She turned back to him, gently kissing his lips for the first time.

"When all was through, what did you wish for?"

Victoria lay on the couch as Truman sat against the base, legs sprawled beneath the coffee table.

"Simplicity," she answered.

He put his head back so it slightly grazed her kneecap, sending a tingling tickle up her leg, between her thighs.

Truman looked up to the ceiling, "Simplicity?"

"Yeah. I no longer want to be the subject of gossip, or the recipient of pitiful glances."

"That's all I got from the doctors and therapists when I was trying to walk and speak again. Each had a tone of pity, as if they were talking to someone who didn't understand a single word they spoke. Alexander was the only one who talked to me like I was a human being; that's probably why he's the only one I associate with now that I'm out. He's shown me the respect each individual deserves."

"And the generosity of housing."

"Another small detail," he said. "Soon I'll be moving out."

"I hope after I leave the shelter things will be normal. A woman who works there said she could get me a job at the clothing store on First Avenue. It probably won't pay much, but should be enough for an apartment."

"I was wondering," he trailed off.

She sat up, "What is it?"

"What was he like?"

"Vincent?"

"Yeah."

"What is it you want to know? You've witnessed his capabilities," she motioned to her side.

"Whatever you want to share."

"I was timid in high school, always trying to get a glimpse of him from my locker. His was next to mine...the girls flocked to him. Cheerleaders. Their short skirts and whorish make-up, probably coordinating times to give him blows. Vincent was a running back, nothing scared him. Once, I saw him fight off three guys at once, the wounded at minimum leaving with bruises. I wish I could catch his face in fear, the prick, it would be priceless. It took me awhile to attract his attention, word had it he thought I was a cute piece of ass anyway. I knew then what he was, but I was too engulfed in his jock muscles."

"What did he do?"

"Mind games. Showing interest to everyone except me. Like all high school girls, this made me desire him more. We graduated and moved in together, then the late nights began. He would come home at one or two in the morning, drunk. Although I was awake each time he stumbled in, I tried not to move. I learned early enough that confronting him in that state led to being hit...and sometimes worse."

Truman shuddered.

"By that time I was too afraid to leave and I had nowhere to go. So, I lived each day accordingly, until recently..."

Truman sat silent for close to five minutes.

"When you think of Vincent, what's the first thing that comes to your mind?"

"Shadows."

"What do you mean?"

"He will always be an approaching shadow. Every night, when he returned home drunk, all of the lights were off as he came at me. I never saw his face, only his silhouette. Many times I thought it was all a dream . . . wished it was a dream."

"I guess we all have shadows of our past which haunt us," responded Truman.

The lock unbolted causing both to jump. Alexander entered.

"Hey there. I'm not intruding am I?" he asked.

Victoria sat up, "Of course not. You seem to be home early."

Alexander shrugged, "I'm tired."

"At nine?" asked Truman.

"All of my energy has been," Alexander paused, "released."

Victoria rose from the couch as she spoke, "Don't worry Alexander, someday you'll find someone who'll last longer than one day."

She walked toward the hallway.

When Alexander heard the bathroom door shut, he whispered, "So, how's everything going? Do I smell the putridness of love in here?"

"Not sure, but you better not smell the couch, just in case."

"Sick bastard. So, *have* you gotten with her yet?"

"Always chivalry 'til the end?"

"When two people have been through what you both have, nothing is too soon in life."

Toilet flush.

"What are you up to?" said Victoria.

Alexander smiled, "Nothing. Just asking if the two of you have done it yet."

Victoria laughed, "Subtle."

"I'm going to bed. You guys can watch a movie or something. It's nice you finally got your own car. Now I don't have to worry about what you're doing with," Alexander paused, "or *in*, mine."

Truman sees headlights in his rearview mirror as he pulls away from the curb but is too busy waving goodbye to Victoria to give more than a glance. The street is empty, the air cold. The lights behind gain distance, rapidly growing in size from small peas to grapefruits.

Crunch.

The first nudge to the bumper causes shock more than anything, forcing Truman to overcorrect and swerve into the oncoming lane.

He looks into the side mirror helplessly.

The lights approach again.

Crunch.

Truman slows, pulling to the side of the road as his stomach churns. He waits as the car pulls in front of him, stopping in the distance. Truman leaves his headlights on, allowing him to watch the shadow bob inside the unknown vehicle. He can only smell his sweat in the enclosed cabin as he sees the car slightly sway back and forth. The driver's door flies open. Everything is motionless. Truman's heart pounds against his chest, wanting to break free from his body and hide beneath the seat.

The man exits the car, his back turned, shielding his identity, only his black hair discernable from a distance. When he turns, he quickly squints as the headlights shoot into his eyes. He is forced to use his hand to deter the light. Truman tries to look beneath, to see the face, but can't get a clear view. It is not until he is almost at the window that Truman realizes who it is.

Vincent.

Truman has never seen a picture of Vincent but the endless descriptions from Victoria have allowed him to paint a mental picture; greasy hair, brown eyes, only wears tight shirts, making sure not to extenuate his muscles. The paranoia rushes from Truman's body. Anger ensues. He faces forward, hands upon the steering wheel, as Vincent stands outside his window.

Truman sees an abandoned car in the distance.

Did he pass a car earlier?

Truman can't remember.

His thoughts are shattered when Vincent arrogantly leans over and knocks on the glass, only using his index finger knuckle.

Tap. Tap.

The movement is swift with impatience. Truman does not move but can see Vincent's eyebrows raise from the corner of his eye.

Vincent knocks again, violently.

Tap. Tap. Tap.

Truman pries white knuckles from the steering wheel. Vincent sees Truman's cheeks harden as a small stream of blood runs from his nose. He backs away, stumbling, almost falling to the ground. Truman runs his tongue over his lips, smearing them with blood and rolls down the window to get the first stench of fear.

"What's wrong?"

It had been eight hours since Truman dropped Victoria off. He slept in his car.

"I saw Vincent."

She fell back into the seat in the shelter lobby.

"Where?"

"He followed me and ran me off the side of the road."

"Oh my God."

"I'm fine."

"I doesn't sound 'fine'…it sounds far from it. He knows where I'm at?"

She stood up and paced in circles, fidgeting her hands and fingers. Rubbing them, cupping them, squeezing them until they turned red . She looked around nervously to every corner and crevice of the room. "I need to tell someone…I need to…"

Her last word trailed to the ceiling as Truman took her hands in his, keeping them still.

"He won't bother you anymore."

Her eyes swelled, "How do you know?"

"He fell back," Truman wiped his brow, "the fear in his face."

She looked up, "Fear? I don't believe it. What did you say?"

"Nothing. Let's not talk about it."

"I don't understand. It probably wasn't Vincent."

"Trust me, it was him. Jet black hair? Cleft chin?"

"And he fell? In fear?" She smiled. "I hope the bastard shit himself."

"Possibly, at least urine."

"Excellent."

They sat silent.

"So, what now?" asked Truman.

"I don't think I need to stay in this place anymore."

"What do you suggest?"

"Moving in together."

"Victoria?"

The drapes were closed, the room full of darkness. Victoria rustled beneath the sheets.

"Victoria?"

The light movement next to Truman accelerated into violent turns.

"Wha...What?" Victoria woke, "Truman? What is it?"

He heard her move across the bed.

"No. Don't turn on the light."

Her movements stopped suddenly, so suddenly, Truman could no longer feel her presence in the dark room.

Truman asked cautiously, "Victoria?"

She whispered, "Yes Truman, I'm here."

"I need to ask you something."

"Can I turn on the light? I can't see anything."

"No. I find comfort with the dark. When I was unconscious there were dreams and Alexander's faceless words but everything was darkness. I knew it was truth, a coffin...after time, I got used to it. It was as much a part of me as I was it. When I woke, I felt like its security was torn from me, like I was supposed to be there, condemned."

"Truman, what are you trying to say?"

"You probably didn't know that the last time I needed to use a cane was when I first saw you. When I first held you . . . I felt the same security I had in the darkness."

Victoria heard a drawer opening. She felt Truman lightly grasp her hand, raising it. He placed a ring on her finger then let her hand go. He sat silently, waiting for her to respond. She did not speak; Truman did not even hear sobbing. He felt her hand upon his face. She lightly ran her fingers over his unshaven chin then kissed his cheek, lips, and finally the scar on his head.

Was red or blue positive?

Truman couldn't remember.

Victoria held the stick out.

"It's positive," said Victoria.

"Gone are the days of social gatherings. Instead we enter shitty diapers, throw-up and sleepless nights," Truman chuckled as he hugged her. "I can't wait."

It was the happiest Truman had seen Julianne, her demeanor soft and inviting. He allowed her to hug him. It was brief, but he knew it took a lot for her to work up such portrayed emotion.

"I want to be the first to congratulate you," she said.

"Why? What did I do?"

"A while back I put in some good words to the community leaders," she smiled, "and a lot of them head the awards committee. Anyway, they were so impressed with your accomplishments, they're going to honor you as the yearly recipient for the state."

"I don't know what to say."

She shook her head in agreement as she walked away.

Truman blurted, "Shit. Now I'll have to thank her in a speech."

Three chandeliers hung from the ceiling, the middle one as large as a pool. Orchids filled glass vases below, each meticulously placed on round, cherry tables, their tablecloths ironed and bleached with no imperfections. People filed into the banquet hall, a procession of tuxedos, glamorous dresses, and monotony. Truman felt Alexander's uncomfortable persona from across the room, until a slim blonde in a black slinky dress passed, checking him from head to toe.

"Taking numbers already?" said Truman as he slapped him on the back.

"Anything to get my mind off this suit; formal wear has never been my forte."

Victoria approached, her red dress shattering the drollness of black and white suits. She told Truman she wanted to take advantage of her waistline, knowing in a short time, her stomach would be too big to fit in anything less than sweat pants.

"Picturesque," said Alexander proudly as he looked at Truman and Victoria together.

Julianne appeared.

"How's it going tonight, kids?" she said.

All three gave accommodating smiles. Alexander quietly slipped away when Julianne's attention turned to Truman. Victoria quickly followed his lead, giving Truman a mischievous smile as she left. Julianne did not seem to notice their disappearance.

"So how are you feeling? Nervous?" she asked.

Truman shrugged with indifference, his stomach clenched.

She continued, "By the way, there's someone I'd like you to meet."

He did not see anyone.

She shook her head, "No, he isn't able to drop by until later. During dinner."

"Coming for the good part?"

"Of course."

He gave a courteous chuckle, which appeased her.

"So, who is this person?" asked Truman.

"Actually, he reminds me a lot of you. He's made some great progress with kids in different community centers," she smiled, "I invited him here so that the two of you may work together on some projects."

A portly man in a suit too small for his stature approached. "Mr. Cooper...everything is ready."

Truman looked over the man's shoulder and noticed all the attendees sitting at their tables patiently.

"I guess I'm on," he said.

Truman sat quietly, listening, but not exactly hearing, the words spoken. He was thinking, at least trying to think, of things to say.

Clapping.

The crowd sat quietly, staring at him.

Truman did not speak immediately, only gazing at the faces in the crowd. All of the chairs were filled, minus one. Truman read the place card.

Jason.

"Looking at all of your faces gives me a happiness I could never describe in words. I find it ironic that you are honoring me for helping the community, because I really should be the one honoring each of you. Everyone in this room played a part in my recovery, and each day, when I went to work, it helped me gain the strength I needed to continue.

"Without each of you, I would not be married to the most unique woman. And I likewise would not be going through the preparations of fatherhood. Now, you all probably know my feelings for Victoria, but there is one other person in this room who I would undoubtedly be dead without. Of course, I'm talking about Alexander. He never gave up on me. After I didn't respond to the world for over a year, he still came into the hospital every morning and treated me with respect.

"I told him this before, but I don't think the rest of you know, I actually remember him talking to me when I was in the coma. Although I couldn't tell you exactly what he was saying, the important thing is that I knew his words were for *me*, which I think was the extra push to bring me back.

"I know many of us have been through tough times in our lives and the only thing I can say is that there are more than a handful of people surrounding you who care. I'm willing to bet whomever you're sitting next to right now would listen to every word you tell them, and more importantly listen to help you, and offer important words, not just blank stares. And when they speak, it will not only be to hear their own voices.

"When I woke, the main thing I wanted to know was the past I had forgotten. Alexander said no one came to me after the attack. He told me not to worry about those who didn't worry for me. Ultimately, he wanted me to move on, because he felt that if they didn't care that I almost died, who needed them? Fuck 'em, he said. Of course, like any words of advice, they're easier to hear than to follow.

"As much as what Alexander said made sense, I still wanted to know. In working with these kids and meeting Victoria, everything has changed. I guess what I'm saying is that most of the people in here are the pieces to the puzzle of my life; although there may be a few pieces which are lost, the picture is still discernable, and ultimately good."

Gerald

Truman and Victoria both gave sensitive smiles as he softly placed his hand on her stomach.

"Isn't her stomach huge?" said Truman. "It looks like she's going to birthe a calf, or maybe quadruplets."

"You never know," responded a jovial, bearded man. "If twins run in the family there's a possibility. Or if you take those hormone doses. You didn't do that, did you? I only think Mormons do that, trying to have more children than China, they are. They've already taken over Utah, what's next? Such a beautiful state, Utah...I once read somewhere that they mass-produce to get closer to God. Have you ever heard such a thing? Closer to God? Is humanity not good enough anymore? Treating each person with respect? As long as you don't murder someone, you have a one-way ticket to heaven, that's what I think. Everything else can be forgiven."

"Robert Reed." The name drifted across the room.

A frown crossed Truman's face as the bearded man said, "And what the hell is with this Christian Coalition bullshit – "

"Please excuse me," Truman said quickly as he turned away.

He surveyed the room. Alexander was on the opposite end with a slight look of horror but Truman paid no attention. He gazed across the crowd until his sight locked upon a younger male, chatting with Julianne, in the far corner. Truman knew the unknown guest had spoken them. He did not hear Victoria's questions of concern as he slowly walked away. As he got closer to the man, the more familiar he seemed.

The walk across the room was in slow motion. Gravity pulled him away instead of bringing him closer.

"What did you say?"

"I'm sorry," responded the young man, "but what do you mean?"

"Truman, this is who I was telling you about earlier," interjected Julianne. "This is Peter Wellington."

Truman, stern and melancholy, did not dampen the smile Julianne had carried all night.

Peter extended his hand as he spoke, "So you are the infamous Truman Cooper. Congratulations on such an achievement, I've already talked to some kids who said they couldn't have survived without you."

Truman was motionless.

Peter looked down at his hand and pulled it to his side, wiping it against his suit.

"What did you say?" asked Truman.

Peter craned his head and said, "I'm sorry, did I miss something?"

Peter looked over at Julianne. She shrugged.

"That name you said earlier, what was it?" asked Truman.

"Name? I'm sure I don't know what you mean."

"You said a name. What was it?"

Peter looked over to Julianne for help, who quickly took cue, "Uh, Truman, we've said a lot of names tonight…"

Truman sternly responded, "I'm talking about one name. It was said a few moments ago," Truman looked toward Peter, "You said a name in conversation and I need to know what that name was."

"Well," a thoughtful look crossed Peter's face. "I was just talking about where I grew up. I'm not sure I could recall all the names I brought up though."

"Robert Reed," said Truman.

"Yes! That's it, Robert Reed," said Julianne. "I remember Peter, you were telling me how much Truman looked like him. A friend from childhood, right?"

Alexander walked up behind Truman, "Hey all, how's everything going?"

"Alexander, could you please give us a moment?" asked Truman.

"Is something wrong?"

"Please. Just a minute."

"Sure. Let me know when you're done."

Peter looked up, into Truman's eyes. Julianne excitedly watched the transition of looks and could not contain her silence.

"Do you know each other?"

"I believe we may have," answered Truman.

"Truman? Peter? Why won't either of you say anything?"

Neither responded.

Julianne exhaled and walked away, head below her shoulders.

"You must forgive me, what did you say your last name was again?" asked Truman.

Peter's eyebrows raised, "Wellington."

Truman repeated the name softly.

"I'm sorry. I do not know you," stated Truman.

Truman could tell from Peter's wide-eye look, that he had just told a lie, an unknowing lie, but a lie nonetheless. A few of the banquet attendees quietly whispered amongst themselves. Their eyes slowly looked at the two, then pulled away.

"Is there any way we could talk outside?" asked Truman.

"Outside? Alone?"

"Why wouldn't you want to speak with me alone?"

"Are you really Robert Reed?"

Truman crossed his arms and pulled his neck into his shoulders to keep warm.

"I don't know."

"But you know the name, don't you?"

Truman told Peter what had happened, leaving out the details of how he ended up in his comatose state.

"It was not until I heard you speak that name that I felt something uneasy in my stomach," said Truman, "a massive churning knowing it has to do with my past.".

Peter did not respond.

"Do you think I'm Robert Reed?"

Peter stood up and looked away.

"It's pretty fucking cold tonight," said Peter. "Colder than it's been in a while. I've only been here for a month but it feels like an eternity. Small cities do that to a person, they make it feel like each second was a day and each day is as pointless as the one before. I actually grew up in this state, in an even smaller town about a hundred and fifty miles from here. My family rarely came down here, few people do. It's its own world. In a town of a thousand people you can't take a shit without having someone ask if you have enough toilet paper. That's why I left, I couldn't handle the constant watching, probing of eyes from people who have nothing better to do.

"I've roamed about the past few years, finding odd jobs in different cities for different community centers. I never wanted to stay in one place for too long; once I was content it was in working order, I would move on. I guess you could call me the catalyst for change." Peter took a deep breath. "This is the closest I've been to my childhood since I left, and yet I have no intention to return to that town. Sometimes I feel that if I didn't know my past life I would be a happier person."

Peter ran his hand through his hair and scratched the back of his neck nervously. "Before we proceed with this conversation, I think you need to ask yourself what good learning about the past will do. You spoke of no one coming to visit you while you were unconscious; is that not enough to tell you that anything from your past probably isn't worth remembering?"

"I need to know who I was. I think it's the only way I'll be able to move on and be the husband and father I should."

Peter sighed.

"You told me you were in a coma for over a year but you didn't say how it happened."

"Two pairs of steel-toed boots pulverized my head, bashing in my skull, leaving me for dead."

Peter looked to the moon.

"Yes, I believe you are Robert Reed."

Truman and Peter listened to the wind.

"How old are you, Peter?"

"Twenty-two."

"If I am who you think I am, how old would I be?"

"About five years older."

"And when was the last time you saw me?"

"The last time I saw Robert was about six years ago, right before he left town."

"Why did he leave?"

Silence.

Truman asked again, "Why did Robert leave town?"

"You know, I'm not the person that should be having this conversation with you. You really should be talking with my brother. He was Robert's friend, I was just the annoying younger brother."

"What's your brother's name?"

"Michael."

Truman repeated the entire name to himself, "Michael Wellington."

Peter looked at Truman's face for any recollection with the name. Truman shook his head and said, "Doesn't sound familiar."

Peter shrugged, "It was worth a shot."

"Does Michael still live at your hometown?"

"Oh yeah, he'll never leave."

Peter pulled a pack of cigarettes from his pocket and held it out to Truman.

Truman shook his head. "No thanks, I don't smoke."

Peter pulled a cigarette out with his mouth. "I guess you quit."

Realization overtook Truman. It sunk in that in the space of two hours, his name, and possibly his future, had changed.

Peter looked at the lit cigarette.

"Death sticks. Isn't that what they call 'em? Why do segways to death have to be so damn soothing? Oh well. I guess we all do unexplainable things, things which hurt us, and others."

"So what happened to Robert's parents?"

Peter took a long drag then said with little compassion, "Dead."

"How did it happen?"

"Died in a car accident when you were a kid. It caused quite an uproar because you were only eight and had no other relatives."

"So what happened to him?"

"Some family friends took you in, an elderly couple. The husband died about five years later. You and the old lady just lived together. You lived with her until you left."

"Where is this woman now?"

Peter again said "Dead," with nonchalance.

Truman's body twitched as a shiver ran up his spine.

"She always asked about you."

Truman looked up to the sky.

"The air seems tainted," mused Peter, "like musk has seeped into the darkness."

"What is the name of the town?"

Peter did not answer.

"Please. I need to know. I promise I won't let anyone know I saw you, I won't even mention your name."

Peter flicked the remainder of his cigarette onto the street as he chuckled. Amidst his laughing, he said, "I'm the least of your worries. Trust me, my name is not the one that will widen eyes in that town."

"What do you mean?"

"Frontier."

"What?"

"Frontier. You wanted to know the name of the town, and that's it. It's about a hundred and fifty miles north east of here. You can either take the highway to some back roads, or you can take the scenic route through Lorenz. It's about halfway to Frontier, halfway to the other side of the world. Most people take the highway though, it's a lot faster."

Truman suddenly realized he had not left the city since he woke over two years ago and wondered if the self-imposed boundary was a conscious, or subconscious, act.

Peter walked toward the parking lot.

"Where are you going?" asked Truman.

"Away from here."

"There must be more you can tell me."

Peter smiled, "I'm through with the past, and like I said before, you should leave it there also. You have a good thing going here, you've helped a lot of people," he trailed off. "I don't think it would be fitting for me to stay for the conclusion of your quest. I think God had me come here tonight to offer you a choice, and I think it's a very important choice. Do you believe in God?"

Truman shrugged, "I suppose so. I think it's God that allowed me to experience life again. When I first woke, I knew I had done things before, but everything became more extravagant. I no longer take things for granted. I think God saved me."

Peter walked over to Truman. Their faces were inches apart.

"So have you ever asked yourself what you needed to be saved from?" he whispered. "It was nice seeing you again Robert, you look good," he paused, "Considering. Tell Julianne thanks for the offer but I'm going to pass."

Peter walked away.

Truman watched him fade into the darkness as he ran his hand along the scar on his head. After a few moments, Truman could only see a small red dot slowly get smaller and smaller; Peter had lit another cigarette.

Truman felt the tension of desired questions roaming inside the vehicle. He was driving, Victoria next to him, no words spoken. Within the silence he felt a slew of questions on the tip of her tongue, causing claustrophobia in his mind. He rolled down the window.

"Please roll that up Truman," said Victoria. "It's freezing."

Sweat upon his brow, he obeyed. When the window was up, she began the questioning, "Who was that guy you were talking with?"

He tried to keep his tone level when he answered. "Whom do you mean?"

"Come on Truman."

"An apparition of the past."

"From the hospital?"

He stirred in his seat. "No, my *past*."

"Really? Why didn't you say anything?"

He cracked his neck in unease as he pulled to the side of the road.

"Truman, what's wrong? Why are you pulling over?"

He stopped and turned off the engine, "We need to talk."

Her voice faltered, "What is it?"

"Please don't be scared. I just don't know what to do," said Truman.

"What happened Trum-"

"Robert."

"What are you talking about?"

"My name is Robert. Robert Reed."

"What did that guy say to you?"

"He said my name is Robert and that I grew up in a town a couple hundred miles from here."

"But," she swallowed heavily, "But how do you know he was telling the truth, maybe he's just trying to upset you. It's known that you don't remember your past."

Truman shook his head. "I don't think so. I'm the one that approached him, and at first he didn't even recognize me."

"What did he say? Who did he say you were, and why did no one visit you after you were attacked?"

"How am I supposed to know? This is all a shock. He only said to go to the town for answers."

"Well, you aren't going, are you?"

He did not answer.

"Why would you do that Truman?" she said.

"Maybe to put my fucking life in order?"

Victoria cupped his chin with her hand. "You're the man I love, and soon to be the father of my child. Isn't that enough?"

"I need to know. I don't want to go through the rest of my life wondering who I was, especially if the answers are so close."

"But what if the answers are detrimental? Your name wouldn't have changed unless something bad happened."

"If it's bad, I'll just have to live with it. One way or another, if I did something unsettling, avoiding my past doesn't mean it didn't happen."

"I just don't think you should go somewhere you so willingly left. You apparently tried to sever all ties with this place."

He held her hands in his, "I need to do this Victoria. Not only for me, but also our child. I would never be able to look at them in the eye if I knew my past was lingering."

She pulled her hands away and looked out the side window. Choking back tears, she said, "I hope you don't get lost along the way."

Truman took the highway straight to Frontier, feeling a scenic route would not be fitting for his purpose. He woke early. Victoria laid on the bed, turned away from him. He knew she had been up the entire night just as he had. After he got ready to leave, he stood in the doorway and asked, "Victoria?"

Her body remained motionless as he left.

She cringed when the front door shut.

Truman drove along the highway with his windows rolled down, cold air exhilarating his body and mind. As he drove north, the patches of snow became more prominent. When the breeze blew onto his face, it was the first time since his conversation with Peter that he felt a twinge of reassurance. His mind cleared doubts and apprehensions. He was able to tell himself that the basis of negative thoughts was due to the testimonial of one person whom he had known for less than an hour. He was able to ease his mind at the thought of returning to a small town, a conglomeration of inviting, smile-painted faces.

Strangers would greet him and ask where he was, and likewise express their concern about his leaving years ago. Why did he leave? To pursue greater ambitions a small town could not quench. Moreover, in reaching such aspirations, he not only had to leave the town behind but also the life he embodied, including his name. Such rationalization bombarded Truman as he got closer to Frontier; he wore a fastidious smile as he rolled into the small town.

Frontier was weather-beaten asphalt and gravel. A handful of early-century buildings spanned the quarter-mile street, the largest a pub with a rust-stained sign, a four-leaf clover extenuating its ill-attempt to drag in customers. The buildings shared a fire truck red motif with chipped paint revealing grey bricks beneath. A lone traffic signal swayed on a cord, blinking red. Truman watched hypnotized. Cars lined both sides of the road and few people walked the sidewalks. A man in a straw hat sat outside the pub, asleep, his pants winking a butt crack. Truman expected a tumbleweed to pass and Yul Brynner round a corner, six shooter at his side. He looked at his watch, noticing it was still early for citizens to be strolling.

He pulled into an empty spot in front of a small grocery store with a weathered sign hanging above: *Gerald's*. The E was almost completely faded. A lonely twig of a tree was planted on the curb, it's dime-sized leaves flapped in the wind as Truman got out and stretched his tightened muscles. Spider web cracks spanned the up heaved sidewalk as dandelions and weeds sprouted from each opening. There was a faint crunch as Truman's heel crushed a yellow bud. A bell above the door chimed. There was no one to greet him. The store was a sliver larger than Alexander's apartment. Truman gazed at the sparse, generic products.

A weak voice from the back startled him, "I'll be right with you."

An old man's head pulled back into an office.

"No rush," said Truman.

"You must be an out-of-towner."

His voice resonated off the walls.

"Why do you say that?"

"Well, in a town this small," said the old man, "a person tends to know everyone."

Truman found solace in the thought of being a stranger to the wisp town.

The man appeared, wiping his glasses with a cloth. "Not to mention, if you live here, you have no reason to be up this early."

He looked up, squinted, put on his glasses. A look of confusion passed across his face.

"You look familiar. Have you been through this town before?"

"I'm not sure."

"You wouldn't forget a place like this."

"That's what I'm trying to figure out."

He cocked his head, "I don't get ya."

"I came here to find answers to questions," said Truman.

The old man's brow furled as he scratched his chin. Truman decided not to run circles around the matter, confusing the man more. Instead, he delved into his questions, "Have you lived here long?"

The old man shook his head, "Oh yes. Very long."

"Would you be able to give me some information about some people that lived here a few years ago?"

"I may not be the best person to ask." He tapped his head, "This thing has been going out on me for a while."

The old man was frail and hunched over in nature. His fingers were skinny straws. Truman waited for one to crack off and fall to the floor.

He started moving scattered cans to a neatly structured pyramid, one can at a time. His joints popped and hissed with each can.

A shiver went up Truman's spine. The movements of the old man were delicate. Flowers opened to greet new days like the old man had the posture of death. Empathy swelled. Truman suffocated tears, waiting for blood to creep from his ducts. He was ready to turn around, exit the store, and jump in his car to return home, forgetting his delusions of grandeur.

The old man stacked the cans and said with slight insignificance, "Robert Reed."

"What was that you said?"

He reached for another and stopped.

"Oh, did I say something?" He shrugged and then tapped his head, "This thing has been going out on me for a while."

The man picked up a can then asked, "I'm sorry, were you waiting on me for something?"

Truman sighed. "Can you please let me know if a Michael Wellington lives in town?"

He placed the can of food meticulously on the stack and said, "Wellington you say? There's a Wellington house just at the intersection of Rye and Field."

Truman headed toward the exit.

"The Winslet family no longer lives in town."

Truman did not acknowledge the words. He had a feeling the old man wouldn't know what he was talking about anyway.

Truman passed a line of decrepit houses, exotic jungles for front yards, gnomes and broken windmills intertwined in the masses, creaking with each gust. Screen doors hung from their remaining hinges and bench swings laid on the porch, broken, brown maple leaves piled on top from trees since removed. Something scurried beneath the green, disappearing in a bush of rosemary as a grey cat jumped from rooftop to rooftop. When Truman initially pulled into the Wellington driveway, he thought the house was abandoned. Strewn boxes and trash covered the front yard and rusted sprinklers atrophied in a spitting motion.

It was a two-story house with familiar red, weather-torn trim. The ends of the roof curled, concaving into the wooden shingles. The drain gutters were filled with mildew, bird droppings and sopping leaves and fresh snow hugged the base boards. Truman released a sigh of awe when he saw the splintered gazebo on the side. Vines covered the structure from the bottom and spanned upward, the stake at the top the only thing untouched. Truman picked up a discarded branch from a nearby tree and hacked a hole large enough to enter without excessive scratches. Inside, the concrete floor and benches were overrun with dirt and leaves; they stirred for the first time in ages with the entering wind. Truman sat on the bench, a layer of dust caking his khaki pants, and looked above. He was able to catch a glimpse of the jutting stake, pointing to heaven.

Small rays of sunlight shot through the cracks in the vines, landing on his forehead.

He sat amongst the suffocating foliage at complete ease.

Truman knocked on the door, waiting patiently for a response. He knocked again. He saw movement out of the corner of his eye. By the time he focused on the nearby window, the drapes were no longer drawn but slowly swaying. He walked over to the window.

"Hello? Mr. Wellington? Can I please speak with you for a moment?"

No response.

"Please sir, I need to speak to your son, Michael."

"Mr. Wellington is dead."

The speaker was just on the other side of the wall. Truman looked through a small crack in the drapes and caught a glimpse of a black jacket.

Hunched over, Truman talked into the window, "I'm sorry to hear that. Are you Michael Wellington?"

"What do you want?"

The voice was further away.

"Your brother, Peter Wellington, told me to talk with you. He said you could help with my problem."

Michael opened the door quickly. He stepped out on the porch, seeing Truman for the first time. Michael's appearance was unkept, his face unshaven, hair long and greasy, and he wore a light blue robe with a large yellow stain at the bottom. Truman sniffed for putridness. The man was relative age to Truman. His eyes widened for a moment, then quickly turned soft and disenchanted.

"Michael Wellington? Sorry to bother you. I'm Truman Cooper."

"Truman Cooper? But," he swallowed heavily, "so you saw Peter?"

Truman ignored Michael's hesitation, "Yes, he was in Asper last week."

"Asper? Really? I never thought he would come that close to home."

Truman bit his lip nervously for a moment then asked, "I'm sorry, do you know who I am?"

Michael looked away and said in an unwavering tone, "You look like someone from my past."

"Who?"

Michael turned back and smiled, moving his body from the doorway, "Would you like to come in?"

The house smelt of spicy mustard and sour cottage cheese. The sun drained through the drapes and dull light came from a small lamp on a table in the entryway. Like the front yard, boxes lined the inside walls. Truman stood still, looking along the floor. The boxes spewed different items: raggedy, age-stained stuffed animals, moth-infested clothing...the one closest to his feet contained letters, the envelopes sprinkled brown from water damage.

"Take a seat," said Michael.

Truman sat down.

Michael sat in a chair across from him.

"Sorry about the mess. I'm trying to get some things in order. My mother died a few months back and it's taken awhile to get everything boxed up. I tried to convince her to pack away some of the stuff after my dad died, but she refused."

Michael looked at the boxes, "My family always had a problem throwing things away, no matter how tattered the item. It's always been hard for any of us to let go of things, but then again, I think this whole town is like that. Kind of depressing though. I think that's why Peter left, he was sick of the dwelling. A lot of people have packed up over the years for the same reason."

Truman nervously gazed around the room.

"Of course, you didn't drive all the way from Asper to hear about that," said Michael.

"I'm sorry, it's just that I'm trying to put my past together."

"Why? What happened?"

Truman once again told his story; the nuances of his presentation were quickly becoming second nature. Michael sat still. Truman felt Michael was purposefully trying to refrain from emotion.

"You think you may be Robert?" asked Michael.

"According to Peter, I am Robert."

Michael grabbed a pack of cigarettes from the coffee table.

"Peter barely knew Robert. We were a couple of years older than Peter, and during high school, years are decades."

Michael lit his cigarette.

"Apparently you were a good friend of Robert's. So, what do you think?" asked Truman.

Michael sat still, slowly smoking . He took a second drag, then a third, watching Truman's anticipation increase.

"Although there are similarities, it's impossible," said Michael.

Truman's shoulders slumped, "Why do you say that?"

He placed his cigarette in an ashtray next to him, stood up, and walked over to a table filled with stacks of papers. He rummaged through them, pulling an envelope from the pile.

Truman took it from Michael's lax fingers.

"I got this from Robert. Unfortunately, we haven't kept in touch. It's hard when people are so far away."

Truman took out the letter and read. It had the signature of Robert Reed. He looked at the postmark on the front of the envelope. Seattle. The date stamp was soon after he woke from unconsciousness.

He stuffed the letter back in the envelope.

"I was wondering if there were any other friends of yours in town I could speak with? Just for my own piece of mind."

Michael shook his head, "The only other friend we hung around with was Eric, but his family moved awhile ago."

"I talked with an old man in the store earlier, he's the one who gave me your address. He said something about a Winslet family. Who are they?"

Michael started laughing, "Gerald? That old loon? I'm surprised he gave you the right directions to my house. You really shouldn't believe anything that guy says."

"What about pictures? Do you have any pictures of Robert?"

"Sorry. Can't help you there. I never got yearbooks and didn't take photos."

Truman unbelievingly looked at the boxes of junk.

Michael saw his doubt and said, "Yeah, you'd think I'd have something but we just never got the chance."

Truman sat still, hoping Michael would say something more; instead, he sat quietly with a newly lit cigarette. Knowing Michael would not willingly offer further information, Truman asked, "One more thing before I leave. Peter made indication of Robert leaving because of something bad. What was he talking about?"

"He probably made it sound worse than it was. A while back someone broke into the hardware store down the street. Cleaned the place out." Michael picked furiously at a small hole in the chair's fabric, "Unfortunately, the only person unaccounted for that night was Robert, so the finger-pointing began."

"He left because of accusations? Was there any certainty he did it?"

"In a small town like this, accusations may as well be a death sentence. It didn't take long for Robert to pack up and leave. I really don't blame him."

Truman nodded in agreement and slowly got up from the couch. Michael rose with him.

"I guess that's it, since you said there's no one else I can speak with..." said Truman.

"Sorry I couldn't be more help to you."

Truman walked toward the door. Michael followed, opening it.

"Well, if you ever come this way again, maybe we can grab a bite to eat or something," said Michael.

Truman's foot hit a large pile of shoes, causing them to topple. He bent down, stacking them.

"I'm sorry about that," said Truman.

"Don't worry about it. I can take care of it, they're all going in the dump anyway."

Truman froze.

"Is something wrong?" said Michael, nervously.

Truman jack hammered his hand into the pile.

He fished out a dirty pair of brown boots, knotted at the end of the laces.

Hunched over, his muscles danced, reliving each blow to his stomach and face.

Subconscious rubbing of scar.

He pulled the shoelace between a clenched fist.

Grunts passed his lips as beads of blood ran down the laces, spreading across the top of the boots.

The boots dangled on the tip of his finger, an offering to Michael. Michael watched as blood flowed freely from a large diagonal gash in Truman's palm.

Truman's gritting teeth echoed. "I guess saving things does run in your family."

Michael listened to the blood fall off the tips to the floor. His tired face stiffened, watching the boots slowly twirl. He covered his mouth and slightly bit his palm.

Truman did not wait for an invite. He walked to the couch, droplets of blood following his trail.

He threw the boots on the table.

Truman casually wiped his hand on the sofa, leaving large smudges of dark red.

"Can I have a glass of water? And some bandages...if you have them."

Truman sat quietly sipping his water, watching the blood slowly seep through the bandage.

"I don't know where to begin," said Michael.

"Why don't you start of by telling me why you tried to kill me?"

"It wouldn't make sense if I started there."

Truman did not respond.

"Earlier, seeing you outside my door, I thought you came back for revenge. But it would be stupid for you to return here with violence on your mind. That's why I believe you when you say you've lost your memory; if you remembered the past, you wouldn't be here."

"Go on."

Michael sighed, "We were best friends during high school: you, Eric and I. We were inseparable. We all knew each other since we were about three. After your parents died and the Neil couple took you in, Eric's and my parents also became your parents in a way. It was rare for you to be away from either house." History shifted, "I didn't want to do it, I never was sure you did what they thought. You seemed so happy. You both had the essence…"

Michael broke down in tears.

Truman squatted in front of the chair.

"The essence of what?" said Truman.

Michael's shoulders jumped.

"Companionship? Love? Whatever one calls a good relationship," responded Michael.

"Love? With who?"

Michael shook his head in denial, jaw clenched.

Truman grabbed his shoulders, nails digging into skin.

"Who did I love? Tell me you piece of shit."

Michael grimaced in pain, answering softly, "Molly Winslet."

Truman fell back. He could not hide the shock from his tone, "Molmy…"

"Molmy? What are you talking about?"

He did not answer, instead, stood up and nervously straightened his clothes. He wished he had not pursued the childish notion of a happy past, wanting to turn and run. As much as he wanted to leave, he knew he could not.

Truman pulled himself off the ground as he spoke, "And what does my past love have to do with you and Eric? Why would either of you care what became of us?"

Michael said, "Because it was Eric's sister."

Truman's knees became weak. He fell onto the couch.

"Sister? I don't..." Truman massaged his temples. "What happened?"

Michael straightened in his chair, "That's where the debate comes in."

"Debate?"

"Her body was never found."

The words whipped across Truman's face. He opened his mouth but could not respond.

"Eric thought you were the one behind it all. So did most of the town. It caused an uproar. Police from surrounding counties combed the entire area but there was no trace of her. They were going to lock you up but they had no evidence. Two high school sweethearts in love . . . that's what everyone was saying. The whole ordeal killed the spirit of this town. It was the first possible homicide we had."

Truman placed his head in his hands, fingers pressing his forehead. When he removed them, red imprints remained. "Why don't I remember any of this?"

Michael slightly chuckled, "Why would you want to? You either lost your love or murdered her. No one was surprised when you disappeared, many were happy. It allowed some to come to terms with things."

"But you and Eric never did?"

Michael's tone became defensive for the first time, "I told you I was never sure if you did it."

"But Eric was sure. The thing I don't understand is that if the three of us were such good friends through the years why would he think I killed this girl?"

Ice clinked in the glass as Michael swirled it clockwise. He quickly poured the remainder of the scotch into his mouth and placed the glass upon the table. The dull thud echoed.

"As much as we were friends, Eric probably cared more about his missing sister."

Sporadic laughter from Truman's mouth increased until he sounded like a lunatic. Michael sat tense in the chair, afraid of what Truman may do.

"Anything else? I didn't beat small children or kill puppies, did I?"

Michael's tension eased with Truman's regretful words.

Truman faded into soft tears, "I don't know what to feel. I can't even feel remorse. I don't know what's truth anymore."

"A great deal of it may not be," said Michael, "The only people that know what truly happened are Molly and God."

"That's not a good enough answer for my conscience. If I never remember my past, that means I won't know what really happened. It's a long time to carry a burden."

"So don't."

Truman looked at him, bewildered.

"My suggestion is to go back home," continued Michael, "tell your wife you had a quiet, uneventful childhood, embrace the birth of your child, and continue to help those in need." He paused. "Peter never should have told you about this place."

"It's not his fault. I pretty much forced him."

Michael waved off his comment, "Whatever, but now you need to move forward."

Truman looked at the letter on the table; the letter he supposedly wrote. He stared at the tattered envelope, "Who wrote that?"

"I did. I read about you in the papers. When I read about Truman Cooper, the 'Man who woke from a year-long coma'…as the article stated it, I wrote the letter in case you showed up."

"Resourceful. How did you get it sent from Seattle?"

"I know someone up there."

"Who? Eric?" Truman could hear the concern in his voice.

Michael pursed his lips, knowing he had revealed too much. However, by telling him everything he knew, Michael felt cleansed. "He and his parents left a few months after you did. If they stayed, it would eat away at them that Molly could be somewhere nearby without them knowing, dead or alive."

Truman eyed the envelope.

"I need to contact them."

"Why? They've come to terms. You showing up would reopen wounds. It would be even worse for you to go up there apologizing for something you know nothing about."

"You're probably right," said Truman, "Could I at least see a picture of Molly?"

Michael reluctantly got up from the chair, "I think I have one of her pictures in my room."

After Michael left, Truman frantically grabbed a pencil he had been eyeing from beneath the table. He tore a page off a magazine on the couch and wrote the address from the envelope. The writing was almost illegible. He stuffed the jagged piece of paper in his coat jacket seconds before Michael returned, who was looking at the small picture, not noticing Truman wiping his brow. Truman pulled his sweat-soaked arm from his head as Michael looked at the table, eyeing the envelope. He handed the picture to Truman.

"It's an older picture," said Michael.

"Can I keep this?"

"I don't know why."

"Let me have it," insisted Truman.

Michael shrugged. Truman held the picture in front of him with both hands, the backside up. Michael sat back in the cushioned chair. Truman's eyes scoured the room. Everything blurred. Michael's face melted into indiscernible features, erasing the acne scars and receding hairline, turning him into a pasty blob. Truman tried to focus. He caught sight of stains on Michael's chair, the substance on its plaid arms slightly resembled coffee, or possibly tea.

Truman's stomach churned as vomit crept up his throat.

Michael carefully studied him, his hands folded in his lap, waiting for an anticipated reaction. Truman felt the probing, uncomfortable wide eyes. He read the back of the picture, 'To Michael'. It was followed by Molly's signature. The simple words pierced his heart. He winced. He turned it over slowly, watching Michael's eyes the entire time, which were fixated on the wallet-sized picture. Truman closed his eyes. Simple, cleansing things passed through his mind. Images of children in rain, flowers in bloom, sunsets. Thoughts were eternity. Eyelids still closed, Truman moved his eyes to the direction of the picture; when he opened them, they dilated from the nearby light.

He had expected a greater emotional reaction. The picture was of a girl, no older than seventeen with blonde hair, green eyes, and a necklace with a small heart.

Michael spoke, "It was taken her sophomore year. About four years before she disappeared. It was the year you started dating. The necklace was from you."

Truman was void of emotion. The girl in the picture was a stranger. Nothing about Molly looked familiar. Lips shut, jaw clenched in frustration, he exhaled through his nose. Instead of providing Michael with a response, Truman calmly placed the photograph into his jacket pocket, fingers grazing the jagged paper with the scrawled address.

"What reason would I have to hurt her?"

"None I can think of. For the most part you were a very mellow person."

"For the most part?"

"It's just," Michael's face furled trying to find the correct words, "there were rages."

"In what way?"

"I only saw it happen once. It was before you even started dating Molly. You, Eric, and I were hanging out when Carter Jones and his friends started giving us shit. I'd say you were about seventeen at the time. Anyway, he started hassling us and made the mistake of talking about your parents. In an instant, you were on top of him, striking with your fists. It took both Eric and me to pull you off him. His face was all bloodied. I never saw anything like it —"

"Until you both did it to me."

Michael looked down in shame as Truman rose from the couch.

"I'm sorry about this little meeting," said Truman, opening the front door.

"Remember that most things in life are tainted, Robert. Water is filtered before people drink it, imagination is lost with innocence, and friends sometimes turn into enemies. Everyone has something they wish they could change."

Truman drove slowly down the main street of Frontier. Below a bird-dropping steeple, two mahogany doors tore open, spitting a crowd of well-dressed meanders, trying to beat each other down the street to the safety of theirs homes for another week. A young girl, no older than five, in a black and white stripped dress, white socks with small pink flowers at the top, and glossed shoes, held her mother's hand. They strolled down the sidewalk, ignoring the people as they rushed by.

Truman pictured himself walking in the same fashion, with his unborn child, and smiled. How ridiculous it is, he thought, to think I had anything to do with Molly's disappearance. I would never forget something so extreme.

The mother caught sight of Truman's gaze. She gave a pleasant smile, nodded, and looked back at the child. Her head snapped back, eyes squinted, trying to block out the rising sun's rays. When Truman was in clear light, her eyes widened. She grabbed her daughter's arm, picked her up, and nestled the small head into her shoulder, hurriedly walking into the closest store.

Truman sank.

Happiness crept out the window and drifted to the sky.

Truman threw his keys on the table, causing Victoria's porcelain vases to clatter. He stood, waiting to see if she awakened from the sound. No light turned on at the end of the hall. In the corner of his eye, Truman noticed a chip on one of the meticulously placed vases. He squatted so they were at eye level. Each was comparable in size but the art varied. Many had floral patterns or angels upon them, but the one chipped had intertwined vines around the entire circumference. Amongst the vines was a tiny rose in half-bloom, struggling to live amongst the foliage, and somehow succeeding.

Truman ran his finger over the chipped edge, a triangular sized piece of the porcelain missing. He looked around the bases of each vase, but was unable to find it. Unfortunately, there were areas of the vase maze that could not be seen without clearing the table, and did not want to risk waking Victoria.

His hand was softly caressing the chip when he noticed Victoria standing in the hall. She had been awake since he left but was reluctant to exit the room. The day was difficult, questionably worse than when Vincent used to beat her. Sadly, it became easy for her to be around Vincent, mainly because she expected to receive at least a few bruises or welts. Whether grabbed too harshly, or slapped across the face, she learned to survive.

When she walked out of the bedroom, Victoria did not know what to expect. The entire day was a mystery. Had she not been pregnant, she knew she would be drunk. She had to settle with unprepared tears, spot cleaning, and chewing of her nails.

"Truman?"

"Your vase broke."

She walked down the hall, stopping a safe distance from his squatting figure.

She looked at his bandaged hand, asking cautiously, "Are you okay?"

Victoria could see the bedroom light glistening off his tears.

"I don't think I will ever be all right."

"What is it?"

Truman reached into his coat pocket. He felt for the picture, pulled it out, leaving the address. He held it out with his left hand, unable to draw his eyes from the broken vase. Victoria squinted but could not see the image. She turned on a lamp, creating a flood of light. Truman's eyes burned. She took the picture from his hand and looked at it, turning it over, reading the writing.

"Who is this Truman? And who is Michael?"

Although it was probably a degree of delusion, the longer Truman looked at the crack, the larger it seemed to grow.

"Michael is the brother of Peter."

He did not elaborate.

"And who is the girl?"

He lightly chuckled, "Yeah, the girl."

He finally rose from his squat.

"She's my old girlfriend."

"I see. And you saw her?"

"Oh, don't worry honey," he said, "It's nothing like that. She's probably dead."

"Dead? How horrible."

"Well, at least missing, but she's been missing for more than six years now," said Truman, "This guy, Michael, said I killed her."

The picture fell from her hand, fluttering to the ground. Truman looked down at Molly's smiling face between their feet.

"What did that guy tell you?"

"Her name is Molly. We were high school sweethearts, and she turned up missing..."

"But why you? What reason would you have?"

Truman realized he was never given a possible motive. Michael only said he beat up that one person...what was his name again? He couldn't remember. His clinched stomach eased for a moment as he began to doubt the entire situation. Even if he had beaten a person to a bloody pulp, would the next step be murder? He was able to think of holes in the story, but he also thought of unanswerable questions. The greatest being why he would go the extent of changing his name, which he felt, was the ultimate step in hiding, if he did nothing wrong.

An act of a guilty person.

Frontier...such a small town...drifters, yes, uncountable drifters must pass through all the time. Molly's an attractive girl...a transient walking the streets avoiding streetlights...a hard-on surfaces under his tattered clothes...Molly walks alone, heading home, tired...the smudge-ridden body jumps from the shadows...he pulls her into the darkness.

Victoria watched Truman go through the mental turmoil.

"...but the way that little girl's mother looked at me. The look in her eyes. She knew I did something, something so horrible she did not want her child to even look at me."

Victoria did not respond.

He looked back to the ground, "I don't blame them for doing what they did, for leaving me there."

"Wait, are you talking about the guys that tried to kill you?"

"Well, yes. It was Michael and his friend Eric, he was Molly's brother," said Truman meekly, "But I would probably do the same. You know, if I was him."

"Are you listening to yourself? Do you hear what you're saying?"

He looked at her, confused.

"I'm not sure of everything you've been telling me, but you still haven't given me evidence as to why you would want to kill this girl."

He shook his head as he spoke, "I really don't know, I don't remember anything. Not the town, not Michael," his tone became firmer, "not Molly, not the death of my parents, or the death of my caretakers. I don't remember being in love before I met you, or relentlessly beating a guy."

"That's exactly my point, Truman. You don't know what happened years ago, and for you to put a vested interest in something a man and his brother are telling you– "

"And the woman who looked at me like I was Death?"

"Still, that doesn't mean you killed anyone. It doesn't mean the past you're chasing is yours."

He responded matter-of-factly, "I knew the name, the one Peter spoke the other night. Robert Reed. Something made me walk over to Peter, an incessant nagging at my mind to find out who he was. Don't tell me that isn't something."

"The only thing of importance is that you know who tried to kill you. Why aren't you upset about that? They left you for dead; they're worse than anything you could have been. So what if this Molly girl is missing? Where's the evidence of you having anything to do with it? You may have, but I highly doubt it, there's still no evidence. But, this Michael, and what was his name? Eric, right? These two guys purposefully tracked you down trying to kill you."

"I lived."

"Just as this girl may be alive somewhere, laughing at all of us, her only goal to get out of a small town without having to answer questions." Victoria pleaded, "Truman, let this go. Whatever happened in the past, let it stay there."

"How can you of all people say such a thing? You, who endured hell, who was so against violence... where are your strong views now? Do they all just go down the toilet because you're carrying my child? What if Vincent knocked you up, would you still be there, happily taking his blows like a dutiful wife?"

Tears surface in her eyes. He could not believe what he had just said. His shame pulled his eyes to the floor. He walked toward the bedroom, head hanging.

Victoria stepped in front of his path.

Truman spoke softly, head still below his shoulders. "Please move."

"No. Did that feel good Truman? I hope it did, because you have no idea how what you just said hurt me. I love you Truman, isn't that enough? If it's not, leave now, and take your past with you."

He nudged her aside.

She grabbed his arm.

Victoria's back was against the wall. She lifted her pregnant body with the support of the table. All of the vases were broken and scattered. Her eyes had turned to fright. Truman was standing above her, arm raised, palm open, ready to strike again. After a few seconds his hand trembled. Victoria remained half-propped against the table, she dared not move.

Truman lowered his hand and put both palms over his mouth, cupping his nose. His knees buckled. He threw the upper part of his body against the floor to find solace. Tears poured as his body swayed back and forth.

Truman peeled his face from the floor and ran his hand over his strawberry-pink cheek. There was a lack of feeling in the rest of his body. He rose slowly and surveyed the area. He did not see Victoria but could hear dishes shuffling in the kitchen. He used slight steps as he approached and poked his right eye around the edge of the doorway, watching as Victoria quietly ate a bowl of cereal. With each mouthful her cheeks quivered. He saw a smudge on the left side of her face, reminiscent of when they first met.

He slammed his head against the doorway. He became everyone else in her life: the abuser. He could not face what he had done, what he promised he would never do. As much as he wanted to console her, he turned and left.

The telephone rang.

"Truman! My life saver."

"What? Alexander? Is that you?"

"Please don't tell me you forgot about tonight."

"Tonight?"

"You forgot."

"Uh..."

"You can't back out on me. Not with this one."

Victoria entered the room, her face placid as she watched Truman sit on the bed in hunched deliberation.

"I'm really sorry, it's just not a good night," said Truman.

Victoria whispered, "We're going."

"Just a second," Truman took the phone from his ear, "What did you say?"

"Get ready. We're going to dinner."

"But..."

"I really don't think you're in a position to argue."

"Truman?" Alexander chimed his name from the muffled receiver; his tone ranged from stern to playful.

Truman sighed, placing the phone to his ear, "What time do you want us there?"

When Truman and Victoria sat down, Alexander looked at her cheek and smiled meekly.

"I'm glad you both came. This is Shelly," said Alexander.

A voluptuous blonde sat next to him, her lips full, eyes a powder blue, an hourglass figure Truman pictured Alexander filling. His sands of time. Truman's eyes were glued on her hardened nipples; he released a brief, exhausted chuckle, wondering if Alexander was running his hand up her skirt.

"So," said Alexander, hands still hidden beneath the table, Shelly still smiling, "I wonder what's good here."

Alexander noticed Truman's blank stare. He gave a quick wink and smile.

Shelly laughed, her lip slightly quivered. Alexander's hand probably broke the panty barrier. Alexander forced jovial laughter while Victoria sat in silence, face unmoving.

"Silence Truman?" said Alexander. "How about a game? I say we all take turns spewing unthinkable vices, weird fetishes. I'll start . . . sex in a wedding dress."

"What's wrong with that?" asked Shelly. "I know a lot of men who have their wives– "

"Who said the woman was wearing the dress?"

Shelly laughed.

"Vices?" asked Truman, softly. His tone increased, "Who are you to talk about vices? Especially when all you're going to do tonight is screw this girl, then probably never see her again."

Alexander's smile didn't waver. He looked at Shelly, at her clueless face. "I'm a man of simple virtues."

"I'm all right with it," replied Shelly.

"See," said Alexander, "We're both on the same page."

"This is fucking ridiculous," said Truman.

Alexander pursed his lips.

Truman picked up a glass of water; his hand shook. He tried to take a drink but was unable to get his mouth to the trembling edge. He slammed the glass down.

Alexander shot up.

"Let's take a walk."

Truman crawled out of the booth and followed Alexander into the bathroom, his head hanging.

"What just happened?" asked Alexander.

"Nothing. I'm sorry...what I said– "

"Fuck that. I could care less about that. I'm more concerned about what's going on with you. Victoria hasn't made eye contact or spoken since you got here."

Truman looked away.

"What happened to her cheek?"

A man stumbled into the restroom. He fell into the door, shattering the bottle of beer he carried.

"God damn it."

The man looked up at Truman and Alexander, "God damn glass bottles."

Alexander's eyes had not moved from Truman's face.

Truman looked away.

The drunken man drug himself to the sinks washing the blood from a small cut on his palm. His body swayed like a bobble doll. He looked at Truman's hand.

"This cut isn't shit compared to that. How the fuck did that happen?"

Truman and Alexander remained silent.

"What? You think I'm a pussy just because I have a smaller cut? Fine. Fuck you too."

He turned back to the sink.

Alexander looked at Truman's hand as Truman tried to hide the shoelace gash beneath his sleeve.

"Fucking sharp edges," blubbered the drunk man. "They'll cut through anything."

Emotionless penetration.

With each push, Victoria curses herself for instigating. She tries to think of her reasoning for foreplay, then remembers reading one of her pregnancy books. Intercourse helps put the baby to sleep. Her stomach has been an internal punching bag for close to two hours.

Truman is turned away, as he was every night for the past two months. It is quiet enough to know he is still awake. His breathing is not rhythmic. It's always rhythmic when he's asleep.

The baby kicks again.

In desperation, Victoria reaches over and caresses Truman's back.

And so it begins.

No words are spoken. They rarely speak anymore. When Truman finally turns over, Victoria has already turned her back to him, slightly sticking out her rear . An invitation. It does not take long for Truman to take heed. His hands are cold on her hips, his lips even colder against her neck. She tightly grips a pillow to her chest, biting it, suffocating a scream. His movements come faster. With time, she feels the climax.

Victoria takes the pillow from her mouth, she can see the tooth marks in the moonlight. Without turning, she reaches behind and caresses Truman's leg, consoling.

"I can always recognize you from your scars."

When Truman looked up from his desk, it took him a moment to register.

Jason.

Truman lit up with genuine happiness for the first time in months. He threw his pencil down in disbelief, "Oh my gosh, look who it is. I was wondering if I would ever see you again."

"Yeah, I'm sorry about that. I've been busy."

Truman hugged Jason with his eyes closed. He did not let go, wanting to suck out Jason's memories so he could feel the way he used to. Jason was accommodating to the affection.

Truman opened his eyes and let go, stepping back in embarrassment.

"Sorry."

"No problem." Jason surveyed the room, "Do you have some time to grab something to eat?"

"Yeah, that'll be great. Did you want to take my car or yours?"

"I'm at the mercy of public transportation right now. I haven't saved up enough for a car."

Truman walked toward the door, grabbing Jason's shoulder tenderly, leading him out.

"One step at a time," said Truman.

Lunch was quiet. Truman ate little food, moving the noddles from side to side, listening to the fork scratch the plate. His eyes were hollow in his sunken face.

"How have you been doing?" asked Jason.

Truman shrugged. "Okay, I guess."

"I'm sorry I didn't make it to your ceremony, I didn't have any way of getting there. I read about it in the paper, though."

"I almost forgot about that," said Truman.

"Congratulations anyway."

Truman nodded.

After lunch, Truman waited in the lobby as Jason made a phone call.

When Jason returned, he said, "I'm living with my uncle now. He's not going to be able to pick me up for a few hours. Is it all right if I head back to the center with you until then?"

Truman thought of the center's accusing eyes.

"I can take you to your uncle's house."

"I couldn't ask that of you. He lives way up in Lorenz…"

Truman thought back to his conversation with Peter, about the two routes to Frontier. Lorenz was one of the two.

"It's the least I could do. I'd like to see some snow…there is snow up there, right?"

"Here and there. The onslaught hasn't begun yet."

Jason fell asleep in the car. As they approached town, Truman noticed greater accumulations of snow on the edges of the road. It seemed abnormally white, he thought, like someone poured bleach over the land, clearing it of animal christenings and vegetation smaller than towering redwoods. The snow-filled ditches were packed sugar, dead grass hidden beneath, waiting for spring.

Jason awakened as they entered his uncle's driveway, "I'm sorry I slept the entire way," he yawned, stretching to the sky. "I really wanted to catch up with you and hear all about Victoria and how you're handling the thoughts of fatherhood."

"Not much to say," Truman responded sharply. "Just drudging along."

Jason sighed as he opened the car door. "That's important," he rubbed the back of his neck. "Parenthood. Whatever happens, just stick through it. My father," he swallowed heavily, "it's hard to look for forgiveness from a scorned child."

As Jason got out of the car he said, "I'll keep in touch."

Truman shook his head. He already had the car in reverse before Jason shut the door. Truman looked in his rearview mirror as Jason said, "I know there's only eight or nine years between us, but you were the closest thing to a parental figure I had."

Truman's shoulders slumped.

"Jason?"

Truman sat still, unable to continue.

Jason smiled and nodded.

"I know. You take care of yourself, and that kid."

Driving back to Asper, Truman forgot the accusations of his past, returning to Victoria with the future on his mind. He wanted to beg her forgiveness. He drove with the windows down, feeling the chill of the air.

He takes a head dive through the windshield and his lifeless body skids into the ditch. He lays face down amongst the weeds and pebbles as droplets of blood escape the holes in his face. Gravel pierces his skin. The car remains resting on the side of the road. His body is not discovered for hours. The only sounds are the idling engine and scurrying of animals. The car takes a breath and dies from the increasing cold. Without the headlights, all is dark. First light comes with dawn. Likewise, it's tourists, looking at the beauties of nature, who find his body intertwined with shards of grass.

Truman sat in his vehicle, wide-eyed, taking slow breaths. With each exhale, he watched the creamy air float above and evaporate into the roof. He closed his eyes tightly a few times, hoping that when he opened them he would be back in bed, next to Victoria. It only caused the vision to be clearer. He struck a white sign, snow draped over its top, making it impossible to read the words beneath. Next to it was a small dirt road leading off the highway into the dark.

He unbuckled his seat belt and rubbed his chest. He left the vehicle running, a noise overbearing the demons in his head. Even with the car's constant murmur, the echo from the shutting door spread for miles. Truman looked at the sign's weathered wood, desperately in need of paint, splintering at the edges, then down the dirt road. It was narrow with faint tire indentations. In between the tracks, weeds and other small plants grew high enough to scrape the undercarriage of any passing vehicle.

Truman returned to his car.

He heard the branches of trees and bushes scratching paint, touching metal. His muscles cringed, stiffening as he drove deeper. Darkness suffocated the headlights. Truman's hands drove effortlessly. He casually steered to the left without thought at a fork in the road.

The minutes melted away.

Subconscious familiarity.

Truman stepped on the brake.

The area around him was the same, each tree looking like its predecessor, the darkness never changing. He turned the car off.

Truman popped the trunk; he could see its faint light in the rearview mirror. He got out and held the car's edge as he proceeded to the back. The darkness of the night was thick enough for the trunk light to pierce his eyes; the last time they were so sensitive was when he woke from his comma.

He rustled through the contents of the trunk, removing a flashlight.

Truman made his way through a towering labyrinth of trees and bushes. There was no path, but he continued to walk. Vines and thorns grabbed his skin, opening small wounds. The flashlight's ray bobbed as he stumbled over the uneven land.

Truman's hip joint became more dissatisfied with the increasing cold. He stumbled and fell from the jolts of pain but pressed on, slowly getting up, wiping the debris from his knees and arms. His right leg dragged behind, a limp piece of meat. The clearing seemed abnormal and out of place. It was a semicircular swimming pool-sized area, containing neither trees nor bushes. He ran the flashlight across the land, past a dying plant in the far corner. He walked over to it, foot dragging behind, painfully kneeling so it was eye level. He broke a piece of a branch, pricking his finger on its thorns. He shined the light upon his hand as blood surfaced and ran down his palm.

Truman picked up the branch, examining it; it was brittle, easily breaking in half. He threw the pieces to the ground and pointed the light at the base of the plant. He reached out to one of many rose petals surrounding it. He pressed it between his fingers, crushing it into dust, and opened his hand. The slight breeze carried the particles into the forest. He painfully rose and unemotionally headed to his car, back through scratches and pricks of contemptuous nature, to the shovel in his trunk.

When Truman returned to the clearing, the sky was brighter. Dawn was approaching. He did not know when he had put the shovel in his trunk, and likewise did not care. When he tried to penetrate the ground, the metal clanged, almost shattering the wooden handle. The area was concrete from the cold. After testing surrounding areas, the only place soft enough was the base of the rose bush. He extracted the dead roots and flung the bush to the side.

Dig.

Dig.

He dug for hours, long after the sun crept over the tops of the trees and his body yearned to stop. He dug as the sweat profusely poured down his face and his body was in such agonizing pain, he no longer knew if it was sweat or blood on his forehead. He did not stop to check. He dug deeper and deeper, all the while finding nothing. There were a few times he vomited from overexertion, but casually dug it out and threw it over his shoulder, onto the building pile of mud and dirt above.

His body, muscles twitching, arms moving slower with each shovel full, felt a strike. Truman threw the shovel, his support, to the side, causing his knees to buckle. On all fours, he cleared the area with his hands.

Robert

As a child, Robert Reed always chose rock during games of *rock, paper, scissors*. It was a memory that resurfaced when he saw the item he struck was a baseball-sized rock. Robert was about to discard it when he noticed faint blood upon it. Although his muscles still ached, he threw dirt above him with cupped hands, a rabid dog scrounging for a lost bone.

Robert's find would have made a dog lick his chops. Inches from the rock was a human skull, shattered on one side. He cleared the area with his hands, finding each bone, lying as they had for years prior, in perfect order from skull to toe. Clothes had since decomposed. He scattered the bones to find clues; a rusted piece of jewelry appeared. A heart. Even in its tarnished display, he recognized the necklace from the picture.

In between realizing the truth of his past, and the lie of his present, Robert fell asleep amongst the remains of his childhood sweetheart. He slept undisturbed for hours, at peace with the surroundings, cradling Molly's shattered skull.

He fell into a spiraling abyss.

In the midst of his dream, indiscernible memories flew past him. Children gallivanting, snow falling... there were times growing up that he felt sleep was the refuge of the imagination. Where else could a person do the things or meet the people they never would otherwise? Men who cannot walk are able to dance; mutes give speeches that make people cry. To Robert, people affected by the beauty of a dream possess a vulnerability which the world needed.

He held her softly in his dream, her remains in reality.

Robert stands in the darkness, the smell of pine needles in the air. Pitch black. He takes a few steps and falls. The trunk of a tree pulls him to his feet. A phosphorescent young girl appears in the distance: blushed cheeks, blonde hair spanning to her back, and crystal blue eyes.

"Molly?"

Robert's words echo.

The apparition smiles, walks away, takes the light with her.

"Molly! Wait!"

Robert stumbles over protruding vines and roots. She is moving much too fast for him, floating above the foliage. He can't keep in the cusp of the glow.

He enters the clearing.

She is standing next to a pile of dirt in the distance. Her eyes are closed. She steps to the side, falling into the ground.

Robert abruptly stops, nearly falling into the large hole. He looks down and sees himself, asleep, next to a skeleton, skull in hands, near his lips.

He felt the world waking around him. Robert tried to hold onto memories which shot into the sky, tendrils of light dissipating through his fingers, remembering holding the girl. He felt simplicity. Logic did not matter. The irrationality of the situation seemed understood. When he woke, all securities distinguished.

His eye opened to the empty socket of Molly's skull.

He forced himself to look at it.

He rose from the hole, peeking over the edge at the sunlight glimmering off a blanket of snow. He could not remember if it had been there last night. Robert grimaced as he lifted himself back to reality. It took a few attempts to pull his exhausted body from the grave.

Molly's bones lay as he met them, in nature's coffin.

He laid on his stomach, grabbing the shovel, then gazed at the leaves of snow. He leaned on the shovel for support as he breathed the cold air; fire entered his lungs. He lifted the shovel and jammed it into the large pile of mud and rocks. He pulled out some of the mess and threw it into the hole.

Robert's limbs and joints were numb. He smoothed the surface with the shovel and replaced the dead rosebush. He left the secluded area for the second time in his life. The final time. Robert buried Molly again but this time took something. He held her necklace in his hand as he walked away. The area he filled with churned earth was void of the tranquillity of the snow around it. Simple flakes started to fall. By night, it covered the entire area, making it impossible to tell what happened.

Robert knocked on the door. He could hear a rustling on the other side. It quickly stopped. He rang the doorbell. Moans and bangs. Cursing. The door chain scraped against the wood and the bolt lock released. Alexander stood in the doorway, delirious, his body swaying back and forth.

Alexander said, "Yeah?"

Robert's lack of response prompted him to force his right eye open; effort was extreme. He stood squinting. Once he was able to register whom was standing in front of him, he strained his lids the remaining distance.

"What time is it?" he yawned.

Robert licked his cracked lips.

"What the hell happened to you?"

Caked with mud, leaves, and blood, Robert's shirt was a pale brown. His muscles twitched.

"Come on in."

Robert stumbled to the couch and sat down.

Alexander went to the sink and splashed his face with cold water.

"Do you mind if I take a piss?" Alexander asked.

Robert was dazed and quiet. Alexander shrugged and quickly disappeared down the hall.

Robert gazed around the small apartment. He pushed on the cushion beneath him and smiled, remembering the endless nights tossing and turning on the same couch a few years ago.

He noticed something different.

The walls were lined with new paintings and sketches. Some of the art was on canvases, others on thin paper. He walked to the array of items and studied each one.

A skeleton tree drenched in orange sunlight, branches like fingers, screaming to the sky.

A red-trimmed house hugging rolling fields of grass, frozen as they bowed to a dirt road twisting to the horizon.

He remembered a few years prior when the walls were bare. He found it strange and empty, but never mentioned it. He recollected the small sketch of the dead women as he studied the remaining art on the wall; he did not see it.

"So, you've noticed the new paintings?"

"They have a lot of vitality," answered Robert. "Warmth. Honestly, I never would have pictured you hanging something so optimistic."

Robert examined a painting, a fusion of blues and yellows melting into the canvas. Slivers of green were apparent where the paints haphazardly met. He bent over and looked at a chicken scrawl of a signature in the bottom right corner.

"Who's the artist?" asked Robert.

"I am."

"All of these?"

Alexander shook his head in agreement.

Robert's mouth curled down on both sides as he straightened his posture, "I didn't know you were into such things."

"I didn't want people to know."

"Why? You're very good."

Alexander nestled himself into Robert's couch divot.

"Did I ever tell you about my mother?"

Robert sat on the chair near him, giving his undivided attention. It was Alexander's devotion as a friend which was sustaining his sanity.

"After my father left," said Alexander, "it was only her and myself. Times were tough of course, but somehow we always drudged through. School to work, day in and out, a monotonous routine for survival."

He took a deep breath, "Everything was going fine until she became sick. Watching the death of anyone you love is agonizing, but the one thing I thanked God for every day was allowing me to know she was going to die."

"I don't understand..."

"I think the process would have been harder had she died with no warning; at least I was able to give my good-byes. I remember toward the end, when she was in the hospital, watching men and women leave after they just lost their spouse or child. Their faces were distant euphoria. I could only imagine having a healthy person, suddenly grabbed away, with no warning, is the worst thing in the world."

There was a stirring from the corner of Robert's eye. Alexander's words melted into the background. In the red house canvas, the fields waved to and fro as a ragged couple appeared on the front porch, the man's arm wrapped around his wife's shoulder. Police cars blazed into the painting, clouds of dust behind, approaching from the horizon, and stopped at the front door steps. A portly man got out of the lead car, adjusted his belt, tilted his hat and spat to the side before he ascended. The rest of the officers stood at their cars, waving their hats to their foreheads, swatting occasional flies, as they wiped the sweat from their brows. The portly man took off his hat and held it to his chest, nervously turning it about as his eyes dropped to his leaf and mud wrapped shoes. He shook his head solemnly. The grip on the woman's shoulder tightened as she was pulled into her husband's chest. A young man appeared in the doorway, jaw-clenched, fists at his sides.

Robert ran his hands over his face, rubbing his eyes.

He looked to the canvas, the fields again frozen in movement, the porch bare, screen door still ajar, an inclination of a shadow in the doorway he didn't notice before.

"I'm sorry I haven't been returning your phone calls," said Robert, eyes still fixed to the painting. " It's just that my life's been falling apart. Since before the incident with Victoria."

Robert could feel an inner thread about to snap.

"I've been under a lot of stress," Robert shifted in his seat. "I wasn't going to tell you, but I found out a few things about my past."

Alexander looked at him curiously.

"It began at the party," Robert stumbled, "there was this guy Peter..."

He told Alexander every detail he could remember. He talked about Peter's brother, the old man at the grocery store and even described Michael's house down to the last bag of festering trash in the front yard. Alexander listened to every word and watched every facial expression intently. Robert felt Alexander studying his every move. It filled him with shame.

After Robert finished talking about his visit to Frontier, Alexander interrupted him, "When did all of this happen? Why are you so filthy?"

Robert sat still. He swallowed the air in his mouth causing his Adam's apple to jump up his throat, trying to tear itself free from the humiliation of a man it was bound to. He started to reach for his pocket to obtain the necklace, not noticing it had been clenched in his hand the entire time. He had to pry his fingers open with his other hand because the blood had stopped flowing, causing it to red and stiffen.

The necklace fell to the ground.

Alexander slowly bent over and picked it up. The heart lay in the palm of his hand as the chain draped between his fingers. "From the picture?"

"Yes."

"Where did you find it?"

"The same place I left it," Robert paused, "around her neck."

Robert told Alexander of the previous night and early morning activities; he was surprised at Alexander's indifference. Alexander responded calmly, "I see…and who have you told about this?"

"You're the first one."

Alexander got off the couch and walked to the kitchen, the necklace still in hand.

"Before we do anything else, I suggest you wash up."

Robert was dumbfounded.

Alexander did not pause in speech, "In the bathroom there should be some fresh towels. I'll fix something to eat. You look like you could use replenishing."

Robert slowly walked down the hall. He saw Alexander from the corner of his eye, his brow furled as he slipped the necklace in his pocket.

Robert turned the shower on before he undressed, the water emitting steam when it struck the tub. He looked behind the door. No towel. Under the sink were only a few rolls of toilet paper and a toilet brush. He left the water running as he exited.

He yelled down the hall, "Alexander…I'm going to grab a towel out of your room."

There was an unbroken clamor of plates and running water. Robert shrugged and entered the bedroom. He filtered through the closet: no towel. He found a clean one hanging on a hook behind the door.

Robert saw a stack of small charcoal drawings leaning against the bed. He walked over, sat down, and picked up the pile. The one on top was of scattered trees in a forest. Robert shuddered when he saw the black-scrawled sun. He shuffled the drawing to the back of the pile.

His mouth fell to his knees.

It was a deserted street with small stores lining both sides. Frontier. His breathing heightened. The next drawing was of Michael Wellington's house, but it was not a shambled estate. It was presentable, a few accumulating piles of leaves foreshadowing the house's demise.

Robert held the picture tightly. The drawings fell from his lap as he exited the room. The steam from the bathroom followed him with subservience.

Alexander cut food near the sink, his back to Robert.

Robert spoke, "You knew, didn't you?"

Alexander did not turn around.

"Knew what?"

"All of it. About Frontier…Molly…and me."

He turned to Robert, his face a prune. He let out a *phewsh* as he walked to the cupboard and pulled out a bottle of tonic water. He did not see the drawing hanging from Robert's hand.

"You knew."

Alexander turned to defend himself when he saw the drawing; no words came from the hole in his face.

"When you walked up to Peter and me at that party, it was no coincidence," said Robert. "Your face, you looked like you saw a ghost."

An ice cube jumped as Alexander slammed the glass on the counter top.

"How could I have known if you killed the girl? I was in the same boat as everyone else. There was a missing girl and no body, end of story. Even when I went up to Frontier to ask people about the incident, no one could say for sure if you did it."

"How…how did you know any of it?"

Alexander took a sip from his glass. "Do you really think the only time you said anything was after your attack? When you first came to the hospital, you were mumbling things left and right, but no one knew because no one cared. Then one day, not only did you pronounce the word correctly, you also included the second piece of crucial information, 'Molly Winslet'…that's what you said.

"I was elated to hear something. I looked up every Molly Winslet across the country. I can honestly say I was amazed to find out the one I was looking for was right in this state.

"My initial intention was to find out her relation to you, and let her know what happened. When I called the house listed, however, some guy answered; he thought I was joking when I brought her name up. It actually took quite a deal of cajoling for him to believe I wasn't. When he realized I was sincere in my attempts, he apologized and told me the whole story. In the end, her entire family left town.

"Needless to say, the conversation was exhausting. When I hung up, I probably should have left things alone. I went to the library and looked up some of Frontier's old newspaper articles. It wasn't hard to find write-ups on the incident," he paused, "And with the articles I found a snapshot of your wonderful face, with the caption reading, 'Robert Reed'.

"So, when I heard that Peter guy say your name that night, yeah, it freaked me out."

Robert did not know how to respond. He swallowed deeply before he spoke, "And what possessed you to not tell me all of this?"

"What good would it have done? Huh? You tell me what difference it would have made? There was no body and you were never convicted, so what crime did you commit?"

"What crime did I commit? I possibly killed a girl and you had me believe I had no past. What gave you the right to withhold the information from me?"

"I felt that you had survived the beating for a reason. A sign of forgiveness."

"You're talking like a madman. What right did you have to make that decision?"

"Who else would have turned a cheek, giving you the luxury of murder? No one cared if you lived or died, just like those jackass doctors and nurses. I'm the only one who cared. I'm the only one who stuck around. I gave you a chance, which is more than you did for yourself."

"But why?"

"Is it that elusive?" Alexander fell mute. He passed a tired look to Robert. When Robert shrugged, Alexander sighed, "Soon after you woke, you said you actually heard some of the words I spoke when you were unconscious?"

"So?"

"One time, ironically it was right before you regained consciousness, I told you a story. A short anecdote. Do you remember?"

Robert shook his head in the negative.

"Well, the story really isn't what's important, only what I realized. I came to the conclusion that the world as a whole is a bunch of selfish bastards. That's kind of an oxymoron isn't it? I spent the greater part of my life trying to do good for other people, and each time I got fucked.

"Let's take you for example. I put all my efforts into getting you better and keeping you alive, only to find out you were a possible murderer. Although you may not think so, changing bedpans and keeping a person's body in working order is a very intimate thing that requires a great deal of vested interest.

"So when I found out, I felt cheated, just like all past instances of my life. When you woke up and did not have a memory of your past, I took advantage of it. I succumbed to selfishness like the rest of the world. I knew you were the only person that could bring me back to what I was before my mother died."

"What are you saying?"

"You were my greatest artistic challenge." Alexander got up from the chair and walked to his wall of paintings, "They *are* good, aren't they? But none of them compare to you. These only took paint and time, you had to be completely remolded from what you were. And look what I molded you into. A humanitarian, a husband... a *father*. You definitely are a masterpiece."

Robert shot from the couch and grabbed Alexander by the shoulders, lifting him, slamming his back against the wall. The picture Robert had been admiring earlier, of the sun and ocean, fell, shattering the frame.

He put his right forearm against Alexander's throat and applied pressure, allowing only a small amount of air through his windpipe.

"I'm not one of your fucking pictures."

Alexander tried to swallow but Robert's arm did not allow it. He could only sputter a soft wheeze, "And what was Molly?"

Robert held his position, but slightly relieved the pressure. Alexander was barely able to grasp the floor with his toes; Robert kept him slightly off the ground, taking pleasure in Alexander's grappling to keep alive. Even in his vulnerable position, Alexander saw the horror on Robert's face from his comment and began laughing. Unable to grasp much air, his laughs caused his face to turn blue.

Even with a blue face, he laughed.

Robert applied more pressure, causing the laugh to choke off.

"What the fuck are you laughing at?"

Alexander strained, "You're choking me because I made you a good person."

Robert held him a few seconds longer in deep contemplation. He removed his arm and took a step back. Alexander's body slumped to the ground as he coughed to regain breath. He coughed as he spoke, "You are better than art," he coughed again, "You are a walking tragedy."

He slowly rose to his feet.

"Did Peter's brother tell you what the townspeople thought of you?" he asked sternly.

Robert sat back on the couch, winded, "No."

"I asked a lot of people, and the main words that came from their mouths were, 'arrogant' and 'asshole'. Think of all you've accomplished in the past few years alone; you saved Jason's life, Victoria's life, and created new life. You even saved my life." He paused. " I was on the brink of death…in my mind…"

Robert shook his head, "But everything came to be because of a person's death."

"Isn't that how most lives are saved? Through death? It's unfortunate Molly is dead but nothing has changed. She was dead when you met, married, and even knocked-up Victoria."

Robert wanted to grab him by the neck and squeeze as hard as his hands would allow: eyes popping out of sockets as he chokes on his tongue.

"The difference is that I now *know* what I did," said Robert. "And something needs to be done about it."

"What exactly is your plan? Go to the police? What good will that do for the people you saved?"

"It'll get it off my conscience"

"That's more selfish than letting it remain a secret forever. I'm sure Molly's parents put the issue to rest a long time ago. The only reason you would see Molly's family is for you. Not them, not Victoria, but you."

Robert got off the couch and headed to the door; he stopped at Alexander, throwing his hand into his pocket. He tore the necklace out, along with the stitching to the pants; an array of coins fell to the ground, shattering the tension.

Robert opened the door.

"Before you go..." Alexander trailed off.

Robert stopped in the doorway and turned to him, "What is it?"

"That night when Vincent followed you...what did you say to him?"

"But how did you..."

As Robert probed, Alexander smiled devilishly.

"You sick fuck. Have you been following me everywhere?"

"If a puppet is not held up by his strings, he falls to the ground. I just wanted to make sure I was there if you needed reeling in. Like at the restaurant. I can only imagine what would have happened had I not intervened."

Robert clenched his teeth, "I told him I had been through too much to believe in violence."

Alexander laughed as Robert said, "But I would make an exception if he were ever to touch Victoria or anyone I loved, again. I told him they'd need his dental records to identify him," he paused. "My words scared me. I didn't know at the time I had such anger, but he must have seen I was telling the truth."

"See. People don't stray from what they are at the core. My suggestion to you is to go home and never speak of this incident again. You came over here and got it off your chest. Now let it lie."

Robert stood silently for a few moments then exited. He saw Alexander's reflection in the apartment's entrance window, arms outstretched, fingers spread, mocking his steps with movements to fictitious strings.

Robert listened to the rain beat on the roof. Black clouds covered the stars and moon. The wind was moving swiftly. He left his car on as he sat quietly, allowing the heat to circumvent. He did not want to get out but he knew he must. He sat with a torn piece of paper in hand. The Winslet address seemed to be an eternity ago. He looked up from the paper to the numbers on the stone pillar.

They were still the same.

Robert did not know how long it took to get to Seattle; the last thing he remembered was leaving Alexander's apartment. The windows fogged again. He furiously wiped the windshield with his sleeve. His chest heaved as his knuckles became the steering wheel, the tendons in his arms flexing and contracting with each thought. Tears melted his fury. He breathed heavily as the rain died, subsiding to occasional clangs on the roof and windshield. He turned off the engine and buttoned his jacket.

As Robert walked up the steps to the Winslet house, the rain began to pour. He did not see lights inside. He looked at his watch: three-thirty in the morning. He rang the doorbell and stood waiting, condemned. He thought the house was empty when the porch light turned on. Robert held Molly's necklace as the door opened.

The Delicate

"Ronald, come over here. I found one I must have."

Ronald scurried across the marble floor to his beckoning wife. Crocodile penny loafers clicked with each step. The echo shot off the marble walls, up to the glass-dome, as the surrounding voices turned insignificant.

"Yes, Mildred, I see what you mean. It would go great in the study."

Mildred stuck her chubby hand out and pointed at the painting, "The sunset over the trees. Perfect."

Alexander crept up.

"I see you have an interest in one of my paintings."

Mildred jumped.

Alexander stood still, hands behind his back, waiting for one of them to respond. He had been walking around, watching expressions, trying not to make his presence known. He could not help from approaching Mildred and Ronald. Such pompous portrayal disgusted him.

Mildred's face became firm, "Yes, well, it is not as troublesome as your other work."

Alexander took the statement as a compliment.

Mildred fiddled with the pearls around her neck.

The painted image was an angled, overhead view of a clear, swimming pool-sized semicircular area, blanketed with snow, surrounded by trees. It was dusk; the sun was about to rest until morning.

"See that bush?" said Alexander.

Mildred smiled, revealing her fluorescent teeth, "Why yes, that was my most favorite part of the piece."

Alexander said, "The girl's body is buried under that spot."

Mildred's cheeks stiffened as her mouth pruned.

"Of course," said Alexander, "It's only bones by now, the earth and worms have already torn the flesh and muscles away."

Mildred stood aghast.

"Head trauma you know. People never survive head trauma, unless they become a useless slab in a hospital bed, waiting to be turned to avoid bed sores and hoping that particular day won't entail pissing of the pants or defecation."

Mildred swallowed heavily. Behind her, Alexander saw a smirk from Ronald.

"Just think of it. Grey matter spilling from a head, knowing there's nothing you can do. And what if it was a loved one? An accident? A crime of passion? The remorse after the body's laying there, dead or twitching and near death, drool streaming from his or her mouth. What do you do then? You can't go to the police. You can't tell your family because they're all dead or frankly they liked her more than they ever liked you. It was a long relationship, there were no public altercations, no foreshadowing of your heinous act. So, the next question is how far do you need to bury the body, to keep the masses guessing but leaving that twinge in the back of their mind. 'That's impossible, he was so kind,' or 'Who could harm a beautiful young lady, she probably just left'. You drag her body by the feet for the mere fact that you don't want blood and brain pieces on your designer clothes.

"Even the petite are heavy when they're dead. Digging is strenuous but manageable because you know your life and status are at stake. Just bury it away. Tuck it in some undiscoverable crevice of the world."

Alexander looked to Mildred's awe, "Of course, this all speculation. Who could ever kill, or have thoughts of killing, the person they love?"

Alexander looked to Ronald, "Am I right, sir?"

Ronald cleared his throat.

"Yes...well..."

"We're leaving," blurted Mildred.

Ronald raised his finger half way in protest. Mildred's eyes turned to small slits. He slowly lowered the finger to his side, shoulders slumping in unison. His eyes fell to his feet and the marble, realizing he was wearing shoes which cost more than some cars, but was unable to stand up to his wife.

Mildred turned her shoulder to Alexander and headed to the entrance of the gallery. Ronald trailed behind, a puppy. She knocked over the caterer serving champagne, ignoring the crash of crystal, motioning to summon the limousine.

"Impressive."

Alexander straightened his face before he turned around. It was a man in his mid to late thirties; he was holding a glass of mimosa.

"I assume you're Alexander?"

Alexander mockingly bowed. "To serve the rich and contemptuous."

"Oh, you are much better than I imagined."

"What exactly were you imagining?"

"Not much really."

He broke eye contact with Alexander, looking at the passing crowds, their awe-inspired faces gazing at the artwork.

"Don't get me wrong, you are ahead of your time, but I never thought the arrogance of your work would show as strong in person."

Alexander's nostrils flared; his fingers fiddled at his side, picking the dead skin beneath his nails.

The man held out his hand, "I'm Reginald Cross."

Alexander reluctantly shook it.

"I've been to some of your previous shows; never could pick you out of the crowd though. Always found it queer you never made yourself known. It doesn't ring to your arrogance...but in the same turn I think that's one reason your art sells. That's why I purchased one of your pieces. Your lack of spotlight intrigues me."

"I'm not one for the limelight," stated Alexander.

"Sure you aren't." said Reginald. "But this show's different than your others."

"Better?"

"Darker. Something's laced into this work. Maybe ghosts of the past?"

Alexander walked to the painting next to the forest scene.

Reginald followed the few short steps.

"These are all pieces of a story. That one there," he motioned to the rose bush painting, "is toward the end." He nodded to the painting in front of them, "This one, however, is the last of the story."

Two men were entangled, one held the other against a wall, arm against the throat, trying to suffocate.

"Kind of violent."

Alexander shrugged, "There's usually violence in stories."

"This story seems inconclusive."

"As many stories are. I *want* the viewer to feel cheated. They don't know how the confrontation ends . . . and they never will. Of course, people can speculate what occurs to appease the devils in heads. I think too many people look for resolve in things around them because few things are actually resolved in life."

"This painting here," said Reginald. "Why does the one person not have a face? I noticed that a few of the artworks here have the same character. Who is he?"

Alexander reluctantly answered, "I want people to know that monsters are not only under our beds and in our closets; they walk amongst us in the simplest forms: human beings. The truth is hidden beneath the calm. They are people that only survive because of the downfall of others. Parasites. Living off broken beings."

"If you say this show is a story, what good does it do selling them as separate pieces?"

Alexander walked toward the first painting in the collection as he answered, "Stories are not always complete; many times you only have bits and pieces; the rest is up to your mind."

Reginald again shook his head in agreement.

Alexander grabbed a cracker from a passing silver tray and plopped the entire piece in his mouth. He stopped in front of the painting.

"Here's that faceless man again," Reginald said.

It had the same two men from the previous painting. The setting was a hospital room; one man sitting in a chair, the other sleeping in the bed. It was raining.

They slowly paced the room. Reginald was able to see the paintings in new context. The next painting consisted of a man sprawled across the floor in obvious agony, a walker near his side; face turned, body tangled.

The third painting was of a man and woman kissing. The woman's face was unnaturally pure. The man's face was away from the viewer, although it appeared he was kissing her upon the cheek. There was a tear in the woman's eye.

"This one is just beautiful."

They returned to the rose bush.

"There's one thing I don't understand about your show."

"What's that?"

"The name...why did you call it 'the delicate'?"

"I believe that everyone is delicate. Physically and emotionally. People carry this portion of themselves everywhere they go, but try not to expose it because it makes them vulnerable." Alexander glared at the painting, "Lest we are not the judges but the judged, because it is the main purpose of people to find faults amongst their peers. Each one of us has to walk about each day knowing that at least one person they encounter will be thinking how something about them is wrong. It could be their weight, their hair, or simply the gait in their walk; people are only content if everyone else is uglier and less than they are. It will never be spoken publicly, but it's true."

Reginald looked at the bubbles in his glass; his posture showed he'd been privy to such crimes.

"Cheer up. It's only natural. The ugliness is not of the judged but those of the judges. I believe the delicate are everyone because everyone is subject to disappointment."

The patrons filed into the rain-filled street. It was well past eleven and Alexander was tired. The gallery was dark, the only illumination from dim track lights on the ceiling, beaming upon the paintings. The atmosphere pleased him. He preferred to look at his paintings in under-lit areas; he was not able to see flaws of his work as easily. He walked amongst them a final time, knowing with their leaving, the past associated would also disappear.

Alexander walked around the room; the only sound were his shoes against the floor. He looked at the painting of the hospital room; he was impressed with the facial features of Robert. Although he was asleep in the painting, the inner turmoil was apparent in his closed eyes and tensed features. The subject in the chair across from Robert's bed was sitting upright in implied conversation. It was impossible to tell, however, because there were no attributes on his face. There were no eyes, mouth, or even ears, only a mixture of colors swirled in chaos.

Alexander walked to the final painting; he thought back to his old apartment, where the final climax took place. He used a little more red for the faceless man to portray the asphyxiation. The color allowed the viewer to know exactly how hard Robert's arm pressed against the man's throat, cutting his circulation. Alexander gave it the exact muscle tone he remembered, making sure to include the fury upon his face. He stepped closer to the painting and looked deeply into it, staring at the featureless man. His face reflected off the gloss paint, temporarily giving the colors his facial features. He stared in silence. His reflection became the painting. He tried to draw his eyes away, but his mind would not allow him. He gazed into the painting, his body tense.

The face of the monster, he thought.

Alexander's body eased with acceptance as a smile crossed his face.

About the Author

Matthew Sanders was born in 1979 and lives in Phoenix, Arizona with his two sons, Jeremiah and Adam. Matthew has a bachelor's degree in Marketing and is currently pursing a Master's in Business Administration. He has written past short stories and poetry and co-wrote a screenplay. *The Delicate* is his first novel. He is currently working on his second and third novels, *Epitaph for the Few* and *Patience for Pomegranates*.

Printed in the United States
54511LVS00001B/72

9 781425 936440